GOOD VIBES

CARA MALONE

LISBON PRESS

Copyright © 2019 by Cara Malone

All rights reserved.

No part of this book may be reproduced in any form or by any electronic or mechanical means, including information storage and retrieval systems, without written permission from the author, except for the use of brief quotations in a book review.

ACKNOWLEDGMENTS

Thank you to Claire Jarrett for being the best editor and cheerleader I could ask for, and a really darn good namer of things.

Thanks to LJ for the incredible book cover which perfectly captures Libby's essence.

Thanks to my fearless beta tester group for taking Theo's game for the proverbial spin.

And an eternal thank you to my readers and friends. I appreciate you more than I can say and I hope this book gives you all the good vibes.

1

THEO

"Oh wow, did you know the expansion pack has blank cards you can fill in yourself?" Theo Kostas asked her roommate.

She was sitting on the couch with a ripped-open mailer envelope beside her and a brand new card game spread out on the coffee table in front of her. This one was called *Escape From Moon Base 9* and it was all anyone in her online gaming circles were talking about.

Of course, that didn't mean it impressed her roommate.

Andie rolled her eyes on her way from her bedroom to the kitchen. "Nerd alert."

"Shut up," Theo teased. "Do you really think spending an entire Friday night waiting in line to get Nat Butler's autograph is any less nerdy?"

That was what Andie had done last night. She'd gotten home around two a.m. and found Theo staring like a zombie at YouTube videos. She'd talked non-stop for at least thirty minutes about her spiritual connection with the rock star and how she was destined to become the future Mrs. Butler before finally pouring herself into bed around three.

Theo hadn't heard a peep from her until she emerged from her bedroom, dyed blonde hair wild with sleep, apparently with the sole motivation of making fun of Theo's hobbies.

Oh, and coffee.

"Make enough for me, will you?" Theo called into the kitchen. Andie grunted and Theo went back to inspecting her new deck of cards.

Not enough people took advantage of the fill-in-the-blank cards – it took a certain amount of cockiness to think you knew a game better than the developers, but Theo took it as a personal challenge. Her mind was already turning with possibilities when Andie flopped onto the couch beside her, shoving the empty mailing envelope out of the way.

"Five-minute ETA on the coffee," she said. "Did I tell you Nat's eyes have this other-worldly quality to them? Like dark chocolate ganache infused with gold flecks..."

"Yeah," Theo said, distracted. "About ten times last night."

"Oh. Well, they're amazing."

"So I've heard."

Nat Butler was not unattractive, and Theo liked her music as much as anyone could like something their roommate played as if today was the last day it would exist. But Theo wasn't a celebrity chaser, even though she and Andie lived in New York City and they'd bumped into a few.

She wasn't much of a woman chaser at all, in fact. All she needed lately was *Moon Base 9* and her gamer friends online.

"Come on," Andie said. "You would swoon if you met her."

"Maybe."

"You should have come last night," she said, dragging herself off the couch as the coffee maker percolated. "I bet you would have had fun."

Tight crowds in stadium seating. Long bathroom lines. An hour and a half subway ride in the sweltering July heat. Theo's pulse jumped up and she shook her head. "I had fun at home."

"You're 32 years old," Andie said on her way to the coffee maker. "Don't you ever get tired of being 80?"

"Nope."

Maybe an attack card to mess with another player's gravity field... Theo was just mentally filing the idea away for one of the blank cards when the apartment buzzer sounded. Andie was mid-pour so Theo went to the intercom.

"Hello?"

"Buzz me up," her sister said. "And make it snappy – this stuff is heavy."

"You need help?"

"Nah, I got it."

Theo buzzed her sister into the building and took the chain off the apartment door, then went into the kitchen to retrieve her coffee from Andie. She was just gathering her *Moon Base 9* cards to put them away when Penny burst into the apartment and dropped her 20-pound wedding binder on the coffee table.

"Careful!" Theo said. "I just got those cards."

"They're fine," Penny said with a roll of her eyes. "Thanks for the help, by the way."

"You said you had it."

"Now, girls," Andie said. "Quit your bickering or I'll have to send you to separate corners."

"Love you, baby sis," Penny said, pinching Theo's cheek.

Theo swatted at Penny's hand, then went into the kitchen to get her a cup of coffee. When she came back, Penny had completely overtaken the coffee table.

"What is all this?" Theo asked.

"Wedding supplies, of course!" Penny said. She took a long sip of coffee, but by the looks of it, she didn't need to be caffeinated. She'd been riding the wedding planning high for about three months already with no signs of slowing down – and the wedding wasn't for another eleven months. "You two are my maids of honor – please tell me you did *not* forget your promise to help me pick out invitations today."

"Oh Lord," Theo said, inspecting some of the stuff spread across the table. Theo was no savant, but it looked like there were at least two hundred different sample invitations there. "Where did you even *get* this many samples?"

"It's amazing what you can get if you're willing to ask," Penny said.

"Or if you want to spend an entire week talking to suppliers, from the looks of it," Andie said. "Ooh, this one's pretty."

"Too floral," Penny said, plucking the invitation out of Andie's hand and starting a discard pile. "There – one down, just a few more to go."

"You're insane," Theo said. "What does Chet think of all this?"

"Well, he *did* send me over here," Penny said.

"Thanks a lot, Chet," Theo said. "I'll remember this at Christmas when I'm choosing his gift."

Andie and Penny laughed, and Theo brought a chair from the dining room so her sister could take her seat on the couch. The way she saw it, it was her sisterly duty to give Penny a hard time about how impressive it was that she'd become a Bridezilla the instant Chet put that ring on her finger.

But sifting through wedding invitations was actually not a bad way to spend a Saturday morning. It wasn't all that different from getting acquainted with the *Moon Base 9* cards – only these were a lot more formal and, tragically, none of them made reference to space monsters.

"How about this one?" Theo asked, passing an

elegant card with pretty calligraphy to her sister. "It's simple but the font makes it feel modern."

"I like it," Penny said. "This'll go in the *maybe* pile."

The three of them sorted wedding invites for close to an hour before they could finally see the coffee table again beneath all that card stock. The *discard* pile was towering by the time they finished and Penny had narrowed it down to about ten *maybe* cards for Chet to weigh in on.

"Is that all for today?" Andie asked with a yawn. Obviously the coffee, followed by a rigorous invitation scavenger hunt, had done nothing to offset her Nat Butler-induced sleep deprivation.

"Maybe you've got a thousand first dance songs for us to listen to?" Theo suggested. "Or fifty different brands of Jordan almonds to taste for the wedding favors?"

"Don't tempt me," Penny said, tapping the overstuffed wedding binder, the weight of which was most definitely going to throw her back out before next June. "I do have one more wedding-related item to discuss with you two. The bachelorette party."

"Planning that already?" Theo asked. A little nervous jitter worked its way through her stomach – wasn't that something to worry about next spring?

"Yeah, isn't that something you're supposed to leave up to your maids of honor?" Andie asked.

"I would, but you know me – I don't want to," Penny said with a laugh. She turned to Theo. "And I know you don't like taking trips…"

The nervous jitter turned into a fist clenching Theo's

stomach. No, she very much did *not* like taking trips, and she didn't like where this was going.

"But this is my wedding and I only get to have one bachelorette party – I want it to be perfect."

"Ooh, are we going somewhere fun?" Andie asked. She was always up for an adventure and Theo was already calculating Andie into her escape plan. She'd go in Theo's stead, simple as that.

"Vegas," Penny said and Theo's stomach promptly dropped about five inches like a heavy stone had just materialized inside it.

"Las Vegas? Nevada?"

"Sin City, baby," Penny said. Her big blue eyes were alight with excitement and she was obviously already married to the idea. Theo felt sick. Vegas was not just a quick day trip, which she might have been able to handle, or even a weekend trip to the family cabin in the Catskills. Las Vegas was a full-on *trip* and it was giving Theo hives just thinking about it.

The airport. The plane that was nothing more than a steel tube coasting through the air. The lights, the crowds, the *distance* from her safe little apartment with the shelves full of card games and her computer and everything else she needed just a few clicks away.

Jesus.

"I can't," Theo blurted.

She pulled Penny and Andie out of their reverie. They were already getting excited about hotel rooms and cocktails and exploring the Strip, and now they were both staring at Theo. Andie looked sympathetic but Penny had a hard look in her eyes that reminded Theo of their dad. He was the tough-love type, always telling her to 'suck it up' rather than let her weasel her way out of the things that scared her.

"You have to," she said. "I'm sorry, but you're my co-maid of honor and I need you at my bachelorette party."

"You'll have Andie-"

"I love Andie, but you're my sister," Penny said. "It's just for a few days – Friday to Sunday – and it's not happening for nine more months. I figured we'd go in April before the weather in Nevada gets too brutal."

Theo's whole body felt too hot, like someone had turned her internal thermostat way up. The trip could be in a week or eight years from now and she'd feel exactly the same way about it – Penny might as well be asking her to go to freaking Moon Base 9.

"I want to," Theo said. Lie. "I'll do my best."

Another lie. She was already brainstorming a dozen ways she could get out of it. Work obligations. Sudden illness. She'd pick a fight with Penny the day before the trip if she had to. It wasn't that Theo was looking forward to disappointing her sister – after close to three decades of fighting the same exhausting battles over and over inside her own mind, she would *love* to just get on a plane and travel carefree across the country.

But Theo was barely capable of getting out of her chair right now, let alone taking all the steps required to go to Vegas and come back in one piece.

"I'm sorry, but that's not good enough," Penny said, her hands on her hips.

Well, that was new.

Theo's pulse started racing again. Everyone in her family was used to Theo's anxiety-related limitations and she'd trained them a long time ago to expect a certain failure rate when it came to following through on plans.

She always meant well, but sometimes she'd be standing in the doorway of her apartment, all ready to show up and *not* be a disappointment for once. But then a little voice inside her head would whisper in her ear, *It's not safe out there.* And she'd be frozen to the floor.

Her family might not understand it, but they accepted it.

Until now, apparently.

"I don't ask much of you," Penny said. "Do you know how much of a pain in the ass it is to carry twenty pounds of wedding invitations across town on the subway? But I brought them to you because I know you're more comfortable here. I do shit like that for you *all the time,* Theo, and I don't mind. But this is my wedding. I want to go to Vegas with my best friends to celebrate and my sister *will* be there."

Those blue eyes could turn icy when Penny was angry. Theo had seen it a few times, like when Andie told the entire middle school about Penny's embarrassing crush on a teacher, or when Mom grounded Penny for a month over a dented bumper that had actually been a successful frame-job by Theo.

She never got used to it when that icy stare was directed at her. Theo shivered and said, "Okay."

Easier said than done – *much* easier said than done.

But obviously Penny wasn't messing around and Theo's well of excuses had run dry. It didn't matter if Theo had crippling agoraphobia, or if her boss needed her to work through the weekend, or if she was so sick she was actually *dead*.

She was going to freaking Vegas in April.

2

LIBBY

"Hel-lo, Mother," Libby Groman said, throwing her arms wide for a hug before she'd even reached her mother's table. The fringe on the hem of her t-shirt rustled in the wind as she walked out on the restaurant patio, a few heads turning her way at her noisy arrival.

"Must you make every entrance theatrical?" her mom asked as she stood and gave Libby a hug.

"You usually like my theatrics," Libby said. "Something wrong?"

"No, sweetie. Have a seat."

"This place is busy today," Libby remarked as she sat down and crossed her legs, the abundance of fabric from her tie-dyed skirt pooling around her. "Even in this heat."

"You should have worn something cooler," her mom said. "I told you we were dining on the patio."

"I love this skirt," Libby said. "It makes me feel like a time-traveler from colonial times."

"A time-traveler who made a brief stop in the 60s?"

"Exactly! See? You *do* get me," Libby said as the waitress came to take their drink orders. Libby asked for a margarita, her mom ordered a simple glass of water with lemon, and the way the waitress's eyes lingered on Libby's clothes did not escape her attention.

A lot of people stared at Libby. Not all of them stared at her the way this girl did, with more than just curiosity. The waitress was pretty in a girl next door kind of way, more feminine than the type of women Libby usually went for, but she was intrigued.

And Libby found that intriguing in turn.

The girl disappeared to place their drink orders and Libby picked up where she'd left off. "I figured this skirt would get an appreciative reaction from the creative types at the museum. The out-of-the-box thinkers."

"The hipsters, you mean?" her mom asked with a wry smile.

"Precisely," Libby said. "My people."

She'd been looking forward to the Franz Erhard Walther exhibition ever since she found out it was coming back to New York. How often does one get to not only interact with, but crawl all over, an art exhibit like a kid in gym class on parachute day?

"About that," her mom said.

"I don't like the sound of that hesitation," Libby said. "You said you'd go with me."

"Let's have lunch and then we'll talk about it," her mom hedged. "I've got some big news to discuss with you."

"You don't have cancer or something, do you?" Libby blurted, loud enough to turn the heads of the table beside them. Her mom was not the type to make promises and break them, just like Libby wasn't the type to sit patiently through an entire meal with a statement as ominous as that hanging over her head.

"No, nothing like that," her mom said. "I've decided to retire."

"Oh, thank God," Libby said, her heart starting again. "You couldn't have lead with that?"

"Sorry."

The waitress came back with their drinks and Libby let her eyes linger on the girl's glossed lips. She really wasn't Libby's type but Libby got a kick out of watching the girl's cheeks turn a subtle shade of pink as she appraised her.

"Umm, what can I get you?" the girl asked, fumbling a notepad out of her apron. She dropped her pen and Libby bent to retrieve it. She handed it back to the girl with a little nibble of her lower lip and the girl stuttered, "S-sorry."

"It's okay," Libby said. She winked, then said, "I'll have the tacos."

Her mom ordered a quesadilla and when the waitress was out of earshot again, she scolded Libby. "Honestly, is that any way to act around your mother?"

Libby arched an eyebrow. "I'm 35 years old – isn't it a little late to start disapproving of me? Besides, you make a great wing woman and I helped you hit on that hot bank teller last week. Did you ever call him?"

"Do *you* ever call any of the women you flirt with?" her mom shot back. "Or is this all just for sport?"

Libby smiled and took a sip of her margarita. "It's mostly sport. Don't worry, I'll settle down and work on getting you some grandbabies eventually."

"You're not getting any younger, Elizabeth Rose," her mom said in a teasing, sing-song voice as the waitress came back with an unnecessary stack of napkins to add to the ones already on the table.

"Neither are you, Cora Leigh," Libby sang back while she smiled at the waitress. Then she leaned across the table and got serious. "So what's all this about retiring? You're only sixty-two, unless I've lost count to a truly egregious degree."

"That is one of the bright sides to being self-employed," her mom said. "You'll see when you're my age – it's nice to have the choice to do things at your own pace. I think I'll work one more year, then quit while I'm young enough to enjoy my golden years."

"Why wait a year?" Libby asked.

"I've got to find new placements for my clients, for one thing. And I've got you to think about, sweetie," her mom said. "I want to talk about your business."

Libby had a sudden, strong urge to find some sand to stick her head in. It happened every year at tax season, once a month when it was time to pay the bills, and every time her mother checked in on the store's finances.

Maybe that cute waitress could be talked into procuring some sand...

"I want to make sure you're on stable financial

ground before I make a decision that would affect Good Vibes," her mom said.

She was a saint – that was all there was to it.

She'd supported the hell out of Libby when she first floated the idea of opening a queer, female-centric adult store in the East Village. She'd pitched in a good portion of her savings two years ago to help Libby lease a space and buy inventory, calling herself an angel investor who really did turn out to be an angel when Libby realized small business ownership was harder than it looked. She had yet to turn a profit and her mother had yet to complain about that unpaid loan.

"It's not your job to worry about that," Libby said. Although she was immensely grateful that her mother *did* worry about Good Vibes. Little details like electric bills and purchase orders just weren't on Libby's radar, and without her mom's help, she wouldn't have had a clue where to start.

"I know," her mom said. "But I also know how much you love that shop and we need to strategize to make sure it stays open a good long time. How about we skip the museum this afternoon and head over to the store instead? You can show me what you've got going on right now."

"Okay," Libby said. As much as she was looking forward to it, the Walther exhibition was going to be in town all summer and it could wait another week. "So, what are you going to do when you retire? Travel the world?"

Her mom smiled. "A girl can dream."

Good Vibes was all closed up when Libby and her mom arrived.

The shop was a small place sandwiched between one of Libby's favorite bagel shops and a yoga studio that let her rent space for the larger events and workshops that drew crowds too big to fit in Libby's tiny shop.

Her mom was a sex therapist who ran her own practice and she taught a lot of those well-attended workshops. Libby was already starting to imagine how lonely the shop would feel once she retired.

She made the most of the space, though, giving Good Vibes a boutique feel with wall murals from local artists and tapestries draped across the ceiling with its exposed ductwork. In addition to her mom's occasional workshops, Libby had one part-time employee, Josie, but Sunday was always a day of rest for the shop.

She unlocked the front door, leaving the *Closed* sign in place as she let her mom in. There were cloth-covered tables decorated with featured products near the door, a bookshelf full of carefully curated works from the *Kama Sutra* to *The Lesbian Sex Bible*, and Libby's pride and joy, the Vibe Wall filled with every buzzing, pulsing, orgasmic delight you could think of.

Libby went around the shop, turning on a few table lamps that helped create the homey boutique vibe she liked. "Well, what did you have in mind?"

"Let's take a look at your books, sweetie," her mom said.

The shop had harsh fluorescents overhead, but Libby rarely turned them on, and now taking extra time to turn on all the individual lamps meant delaying an uncomfortable conversation. Her accounting files weren't much to see.

Finally, when there were no more lighting adjustments to be made and nothing else to distract her, Libby went behind the checkout counter and turned on the computer that doubled as her cash register. She waved her mom over, then pulled up the sparsely filled spreadsheet that was 'the books'.

"What do you want to know?"

"It's not an interrogation," her mom said, rubbing Libby's back. "I'm not the IRS. Relax – I just want to know how you're doing."

"I'm not the best bookkeeper in the world," Libby said, pushing the computer screen toward her mother. "I try but you know I don't have a mind for details."

Her mom frowned at the screen. She scrolled for a few minutes, frowning some more, then sighed. "Well, you're right about that. There's not much here."

"Josie records the expenses once a month," Libby said. "And she's trying to get me in the habit of tracking a few more statistics but I just never understand the point of it – what am I saving all this data *for*?"

"We really ought to get you into some small business classes," her mom suggested. "You've got all the ingenuity and passion you need to drum up business, and that's the hard part. Statistics and bookkeeping are skills that can be learned."

"Those cost money," Libby pointed out. "And I'd have to be away from the shop more. I'm not sure how many more hours a week I can afford to pay Josie."

"Not many, by the looks of this," her mom said. "Your sales have been stagnating for the last couple of months, according to these numbers."

"You can't always be in a growth cycle, right?"

"That's true, but you can't sustain a business with flat sales," her mom said.

"Well, bookkeeping is only half the problem," Libby said. "People don't like buying their dildos from a place that requires them to take their veiny cocks home on the subway. The online retailers are crushing brick and mortar sex shops."

"That's nothing new," her mom pointed out. "Sweetie, you know I've been happy to help you out with the rent when you need it, and I'd be happy to keep teaching workshops now and then after I retire if it'll bring in new customers. It's not easy getting a small business off the ground and we both knew this would be a journey. Whether there are online retailers gunning for you or not, success requires creativity. That's one of your best qualities, though. Just look at all the customer reviews people have left on the Vibe Wall since you started putting Post-it notes and pens over there. That was a stroke of genius."

"Pun intended," Libby smirked.

Her mom smiled, but she would not be deterred from her concerns, even with the perfect dirty joke. "When I retire, I'm going to be on a fixed income and I won't be able to help out as much as I do now. You'll be on your own."

Libby's heart gave a little jump in her chest. That was the first thing her mom had said all day that truly hit home and it struck fear into her. She didn't know the first thing about the business end of her shop and she'd been taking her mother's generosity – and Josie's enthusiasm for grunt work – for granted since Good Vibes opened.

Could she even do this on her own?

"Don't worry," her mom said, noticing the fear in her eyes. "I'm not planning to leave you high and dry. I'll help however I can."

Libby put her forearms on the counter and blew her hair out of her face. It was blue at the moment, but the color was beginning to fade and she'd been thinking about going purple. That decision barely registered on her priority list now.

"You probably shouldn't have babied me this whole time," she teased. "I'm spoiled now."

"That's a mother's prerogative but it's time to leave the nest, little birdie."

Libby sighed. "I don't know the first thing about balance sheets and inventory control... I don't even know if those are real terms or something I just made up."

She was being melodramatic, but only a little. Her mom laughed and turned off the computer. "I have faith in you, sweetie."

3

THEO

It was a sunny Friday evening and there were a lot of people on the sidewalks. Theo stuck close to Andie, a fake smile plastered on her face as she wondered how the hell she'd been hoodwinked into going on this little adventure.

"It'll just be a quick trip," Andie had promised when she'd grabbed Theo by the hand and physically hauled her off the couch. "You're starting to scare the neighbor kids with your vampiric complexion."

"Maybe I'm trying to be Goth," Theo shot back.

"It doesn't suit you."

"Harsh."

In the end, Andie had won. She had a few good points – including one about a Theo-shaped indent in the couch cushions – and she promised it would be a quick trip. She was taking her responsibilities as co-maid of honor very seriously and she'd begun planning the bachelorette party almost from the moment Penny left the apartment last weekend.

"What's so special about this place again?" Theo asked as they weaved their way up the sidewalk like two fish swimming against the rest of the school.

What she meant to say was, *Why can't we just buy this stuff online?* Or better yet, *Why are we shopping almost a year in advance?* Theo had a litany of questions that all revolved around her pounding heart's insistence that it was better to just go home. But Andie was persistent – she wanted to shop in person and she needed her co-maid of honor to come with her.

"It's a female-centric sex shop," she said. "And I heard they're doing a special feature on bachelorette favors this month – we're just getting ideas at this point, but I thought it would be fun to poke around." She looked at Theo, who gave her an unconvincing smile, and squeezed her hand. "We won't be long – it's a small shop."

"Okay."

That made Theo feel a little better. She could get through anything for twenty minutes and they were already most of the way to their destination anyway. Twenty minutes to make Andie happy seemed like a good trade-off for spending the rest of the weekend cocooned in the safety of the apartment.

"Here it is," Andie said, pulling Theo over to a little shop with big, pink neon letters flashing in the window. "Good Vibes."

Theo snorted as Andie pushed the door open and a

bell chimed to announce them. She was not the type of person to visit a sex shop in the first place and as she walked through the door, the first thing her eyes went to was a mannequin wearing an obscenely big, floppy strap-on.

"Oh, Lord."

"Loosen up," Andie said. "Or I'll make it my job to embarrass you."

"Please don't."

"Oh look, honey," she said loudly, turning a few heads as she plucked a toy off the nearest table. "Didn't you say you wanted to try a bigger butt plug?"

"Not today, dear," Theo said through gritted teeth. She made accidental eye contact with a blue-haired girl from across the shop, promptly turned tomato-red, and Andie laughed like she'd just discovered her own comedic genius.

"Come on," Andie said, setting the butt plug down and leading Theo through the store. "Looks like the bachelorette stuff is on those tables."

There were three tables in the middle of the store with bright pink tablecloths and all manner of yonnic and phallic party favors spread across them. Andie and Theo didn't make it to those tables, though. Andie took about five steps into the store, noticed a massive wall of vibrators and got thoroughly distracted.

"Holy shit, this is amazing." She picked something up, it started buzzing, and Theo looked away, accidentally locking eyes with the blue-haired girl again.

She smiled at Theo – was that flirtatious or just

friendly? Then the girl turned, her purple crinoline skirt floating around her like a cloud, and plucked a book from a large shelf.

"You might like this one," she said to the woman standing next to her. Theo realized she must work there as she added with a wink, "Some of the sitting positions are *very* creative."

"How do you feel about the Cone?" Andie asked, nudging Theo. "Total gimmick, or could it possibly feel good?"

"The what?"

"This thing." She was holding a pink, vibrating toy that looked just like it sounded – a smooth cone a little bigger than the palm of Andie's hand, with an unsettlingly pointy tip.

"What the hell do you do with it?" Theo asked.

"Umm..." Andie referred back to the wall of toys, where Post-it notes were stuck haphazardly near the toys to which they referred. "Sit on it?"

Theo laughed. "You first."

"You're so old-fashioned," Andie said, turning off the Cone and putting it back on the shelf.

"My hands do the job just fine and they're free," Theo said. "Can we please go look at what we came here for?"

By her count, they'd been at Good Vibes for about five minutes – fifteen more to go, then Theo's obligation would be fulfilled. She always felt better when she was leaving a place – like how she could never enjoy a roller coaster while she was actually on the ride because her anxiety about how it was going to go took up every inch of space inside her mind.

After it was over and the adrenaline had been spent, she could look back and appreciate the experience in hindsight. And she was very much looking forward to putting Good Vibes in her rear view mirror.

Andie rolled her eyes. "I didn't come all the way out to the East Village to look at booby gummy candy for five seconds and go home. Browse with me for a few minutes, okay?"

Being a wet blanket was no fun, and yet it was something Theo rarely had the power to control. She took a deep breath and resolved to try – at least for the next fifteen minutes.

"Okay."

"I'm going to go check out the books," Andie said, leaving Theo stranded at the wall of variously shaped things that go inside you.

She was just looking around for a safe escape when the blue-haired girl popped up beside her and loudly said, "Hello!"

Theo nearly jumped out of her skin. "Hi."

"What do you think of the Vibe Wall?" she asked. "Find anything you like?"

"Umm, my friend was looking at the Cone."

"Interesting choice," the girl said. Up close, she had the most stunning eyes, like polished gray stone, and they never left Theo's face. "The Cone is a unique sensation, but it's a bit of a one-trick pony. I prefer something a little more versatile."

"You've tried it?"

"I've tried most of the toys on the Vibe Wall," the girl said. "Otherwise how could I recommend the right toy for you?"

"I'm not here for a toy," Theo quickly corrected, looking from those polished stone eyes to the girl's puffy skirt, which brushed against Theo's legs every time she moved.

"No judgment," she said. "That's my motto. I'm Libby, by the way. Owner, operator, sex toy aficionado."

She held out her hand and Theo took it, introducing herself as well.

Libby let the handshake linger until Theo's cheeks started to burn beneath her gaze and Libby blurted, "You've got great lips. Did you know that?"

Theo smiled. "Yeah, actually, that's what my boss put on my last performance evaluation. 'Great lips'."

Libby smiled back at her. She didn't have such bad lips herself and her smile sure was charming. "Your boss said that? Not your boyfriend... or girlfriend?"

"None of the above for me," Theo said.

"Well, at least *someone's* appreciating your lips," Libby said. "So what brings you into Good Vibes?"

Theo had to struggle to keep from blurting out something along the lines of, *Oh, Lord, definitely not the Vibe Wall*. Instead, she said, "My sister's getting married and I guess that means we need a bunch of dick-shaped pasta or something for the bachelorette party."

Libby frowned. "I'm not sure we have any dick-shaped pasta."

"I was joking-"

"This is why the big online retailers are killing small business," she said. "I bet you're going to go home and get all your erotic pasta needs fulfilled by drone now."

Theo broke Libby's gaze. That was *exactly* what she'd been thinking on the way to the shop but now that she'd met the owner, she was feeling guilty about it. "No-"

"It's okay," Libby said. "But maybe I can interest you in a 'Bride to Be' sash or a naughty piñata?"

She grabbed Theo's hand and led her over to the bachelorette tables. Theo's head was swimming while she tried to orient herself to this surprising girl. On the long list of all the things Theo thought could happen on this trip, being led through the shop by a blue-haired beauty who wasn't shy about sharing her sex toy experiences was *not* on Theo's radar.

Andie joined them at the table and Libby proved to be just as knowledgeable about her bachelorette offerings as she was about the Vibe Wall. Theo listened quietly – there had never been a point in her life that she didn't know Penny, but that didn't mean Theo had the first clue about what sorts of cheesy bachelorette accessories she might want to traipse around Las Vegas in, so she left those decisions to Andie.

What Theo did notice, while Libby explained the functional benefits of a so-called 'willy shot glass' in limiting alcohol consumption, was that she felt quite a bit calmer now. The anxiety that had been inching its way up to a seven out of ten while she and Andie navigated the sidewalks was now down to a rather manageable three, and it seemed to have something to do with Libby.

She was bewitching, in a pretty literal sense.

"Theo?"

"Huh?"

Andie was looking at her. Libby was, too. And she'd been absorbed in the mesmerizing motion of Libby's mouth as she talked about her bachelorette products.

"I asked if you think Penny would like the willy shot glass," Andie repeated.

Theo shrugged, looking again at the little pink phallus molded into the bottom of the cup. "Straight girls, am I right?"

It was all she could think to say, but Andie and Libby both laughed. There was that look again, and the pleasant warmth of being under Libby's gaze. Perhaps there was something to be said for going shopping in the real world after all – you couldn't get that feeling delivered via drone.

"Maybe we'll put a pin in the shot glass then," Libby suggested. "What else can I show you?"

"I simply *must* get a pack of booby balloons," Andie said. "Not for Penny – just for apartment décor. Don't you think, Theo?"

"You know me," she said. "I'm never opposed to boobs."

"Then it's settled," Andie said, taking a package from Libby. "And we'll be sure to come back closer to the date to load up on all the bachelorette supplies we need."

Libby led them over to the counter and while she

rang up the balloons, Andie got out her phone. "Come here, Theo. I need photographic proof that I got you to come to a sex shop."

Theo rolled her eyes, but it was a good thing that Andie had appointed herself the group photographer. Otherwise, Theo would probably have about three photos of herself – it just wasn't something she thought to do, but Andie excelled at all forms of social documentation.

She'd probably need a whole extra storage card in her phone for the Vegas trip. She snapped four photos before she finally put down her phone and gave Libby her credit card for the balloons.

"It'll just be a minute," Libby said. "I haven't quite figured out how to send receipts to the printer automatically and it takes a second to warm up."

"No worries," Andie said. "I'm just going to check out your lube selection while I wait."

She went over to a small rack beside the door and Libby leaned across the counter to Theo. "While we have a little time to kill, I thought I would ask for your number. That is, unless I was misreading you?"

Theo's mouth dropped open slightly. Suddenly her anxiety was back up to a six and her mind was racing its way through every little thing that could happen if she gave her number to this blue-haired beauty. Who just *asked* for someone's number after knowing them for ten minutes, anyway?

Libby noticed her hesitation and stood upright again. "Or not. No pressure."

Her words were casual but there was a little bit of hurt in her eyes. Theo hadn't known the pain of rejection for years because she steadfastly refused to open herself up to it, but the distant memory of what it felt like was not a good one.

"I would," she hurried to explain, "but I don't date."

It wasn't a lie, but it didn't seem to soften the blow at all. Libby said, "Oh."

She looked crushed, like she was taking this personally. Theo stole a glance in Andie's direction. She was watching the whole exchange and looking judgmentally at her. She turned back to Libby. "You're very pretty-"

"No need to explain," Libby said. The bell above the door jingled and she called, "Welcome to Good Vibes!" then grabbed Andie's receipt off the printer and handed it to Theo with a plastic smile. "Have a great day – good luck with that bachelorette party."

Theo had the urge to apologize but Libby was already on her way over to greet her new customers. Theo handed the receipt to Andie, preemptively cutting her off. "Don't say anything."

"But why'd you turn her down?" Andie whined as they headed outside. "She liked you. And from where I was standing, it sure looked like you liked her, too."

"It's not that simple."

"It could be."

"It's not."

If a twenty-minute trip to the East Village brought Theo into a state of near panic, how could she ever manage the thousands of steps to go from giving a girl her number to going on a date or whatever else that might entail? It was too much and it would only lead to disappointment – for Theo and Libby both.

It was better to get the disappointment out of the way now and be done with it.

"Come on," she said. "We've got booby balloons to blow up."

"Can we fill the balcony with them like it's a ball pit?"

"We could fill a closet instead," Theo suggested. "And turn it into a booby trap."

Andie slung her arm over Theo's shoulder. "I like how you think."

4

LIBBY

Libby arrived at Good Vibes bright and early the next morning. The shop didn't open until ten a.m. on Saturdays and most of the time, she breezed in at the last minute, turned on the lights, flipped the sign in the window and called it good.

Today, she let herself in at about a quarter to nine and went into the small office behind the check-out counter to brew herself a strong pot of coffee. She was wearing her most business-womanly structured suit jacket (with a turquoise pleated mini skirt layered beneath it), and she was ready to get down to business.

After the coffee finished brewing.

And the spider plants hanging in the windows were watered.

And the featured table displays were tidied up. She couldn't very well open up shop on the busiest day of the week with disorderly dildos, could she?

But after all those distracting, very important tasks

were completed, Libby took her coffee cup over to the computer, cracked her knuckles and sat down to work. She now had just fifty-one weeks to come to terms with all the aspects of her business that she'd had the luxury of ignoring for the last two years – balance sheets, profit and loss reports, advertising campaigns, strategic plans...

"What the heck *is* a strategic plan?" she asked the empty shop, or maybe the question was directed at the spider plants.

In any case, Libby didn't receive an answer. All she knew for sure was that she couldn't bear it if her mother's faith and trust in her turned out to be misplaced.

"I will not drive this place into the ground," Libby announced to the plants. "Mark my words."

She was just giving herself a quick, Google-based education in strategic planning – something about setting goals and allocating resources that left Libby feeling a bit dizzy and overwhelmed – when someone rapped on the glass pane of the door.

"We're closed," Libby called, but when she looked up, she recognized her precocious visitor. It was that handsome soft butch from yesterday – the one with the great lips.

The one who'd rejected her.

Libby looked back at her computer screen. '...*an organization's process of defining its strategy*...'

"Oh, to hell with that," she said, sliding off her stool and adopting the slightly coy smile that always served her well with the ladies. She unlocked the door and draped herself across the doorframe. "Hey there, stranger. We're not open for another hour, you know."

"Yeah, I realized that on the subway over here," Theo said. "Sorry. I'm glad you're here, though."

"Oh yeah?" Libby raised an eyebrow at Theo. Maybe she was rethinking that whole 'no dating' thing after all.

"My friend thinks she left her phone on the counter yesterday."

"Oh." Libby tried not to let the disappointment show on her face. "Come in – I didn't notice a phone, but I'm not really a details kind of person."

"Thanks," Theo said. As she slid past her in the doorway, Libby caught a waft of her smell – clean and ever so slightly masculine, like Ivory soap. Her short hair was slicked back and it was slightly wavy, like she'd let it air-dry in the muggy July heat.

"Help yourself," Libby said. She locked the door behind Theo lest anyone else mistake this as an invitation to start shopping, then met her at the counter. Theo already had the phone in her hand.

"Right where Andie said it would be," she said. "You know, I have a strong suspicion that she left it here on purpose."

"For that sweet, sweet property insurance money?"

Theo laughed. "That, and because she fancies herself a bit of a matchmaker."

"Otherwise she could have just come by and picked it up herself," Libby agreed. "How are those booby balloons treating you, by the way?"

"Oh, they're great. Tits as far as the eye can see."

"That's all any of us wants in life, right?" Libby teased. "Well, maybe not *you.*"

Did Theo really not date or had she just been blowing Libby off? She was probably patiently waiting for Libby to unlock the door and let her get the hell out of there.

"I'm sorry about yesterday," Theo said.

"There's no need to apologize-"

"Yeah, there is," Theo answered, slipping the phone into her back pocket. "I was rude and I didn't mean to be. If things were different, I would actually really like to take you out sometime. You seem really interesting."

"If things were different? What, you have a girlfriend or something?"

"No," Theo said quickly. She was picking at her fingernails and she didn't look very comfortable. Libby had a way of accidentally pushing people's buttons. Theo sighed and asked, "Do you know what agoraphobia is?"

"Fear of the Dixie Chicks?" Libby asked, and when this failed to get a laugh, she added, "You know, because of their song, *Wide Open Spaces*? Sorry, bad joke."

"It's okay," Theo said, although she still wasn't laughing. "For some agoraphobics, it's wide open spaces. For others, it's more general – anyplace where you feel like you can't easily escape if you need to." She sighed again. "Anyway, I have that and I was kinda freaking out yesterday when you asked for my number."

"So I guess I shouldn't have locked the door just now," Libby said. "Is it bothering you?"

"I'm okay," Theo said. "If I asked to leave, you'd let me out... right?"

"Well, I've got a lot of bondage ropes here but I promise not to use them unless you ask me to." Libby thought better of the joke just as the words escaped her lips, but Theo actually laughed at that one.

"Thanks for not making too big a deal out of it," Theo said. "I don't tell many people but I felt like I owed you an explanation."

"You don't owe me anything. But if you want to stick around a few more minutes, I could get you a cup of coffee."

Theo considered it, and just when Libby thought she was about to make a run for the door, she said, "Sure."

"How do you take it?"

"Sugar, no creamer. Thanks."

Libby went back into the office and borrowed Josie's coffee cup – the rainbow one with *Does this mug make me look gay?* printed across it. When she came back around the counter, she handed it to Theo and asked, "So what do you think would happen if you couldn't escape? Is that too nosy?"

"It's not," Theo said. "But I don't have a handy answer. It's one of those *impending sense of doom* things – I always think something bad is going to happen, but it changes based on the situation. When I was a kid, I used to get carsick pretty much every time my family went on a trip, and between actual nausea and racing, anxious thoughts, I guess it just kind of forged neural pathways in my brain. Going too far from home equals sickness and other bad things."

"Sounds traumatic."

Theo just shrugged. She took a sip of coffee, noticed the wording on the mug and smirked. "Good coffee, great mug."

"Thanks. You know, I was a bit of a homebody as a kid myself."

"Oh yeah?"

"If you looked up the phrase 'painfully shy,' you would have found a picture of my face," Libby said. Theo's mouth dropped open and she laughed.

"You? Painfully shy?" Theo was looking at the turquoise miniskirt and the dozen bangle bracelets stacked on Libby's wrist, then her eyes made their way up to the faded blue of Libby's hair as she said, "I can't believe it."

"It's true," Libby said. "I spent most of my formative years hiding out in my room, making friends on the Internet. That's where I met my best friend, Robin. She had a lot of influence into all of this." She gave her bangles a little shake, gestured to her wild-colored hair, and smiled. "Robin used to have a fearless sense of fashion and it rubbed off on me."

"You seem pretty fearless in your own right."

Libby told Theo about the time in middle school when Robin convinced her to wear faux fur cat ears to class. Robin lived in Toronto and she and Libby video chatted almost every day, and they'd already taken to wearing the cat ears in their respective bedrooms. It had taken an entire week of convincing before Robin talked Libby into wearing them outside the house.

"The other kids already hate us at worst, ignore us at best," Robin had argued. She was wearing her ears at the time and they *did* look cute on her. "If they're going to exclude us either way, why not do what makes us feel good?"

Robin always was persuasive, even through a computer screen, and she pretty much always got her way where Libby was concerned. Who could say no to a cute girl in cat ears? So Libby went to school the next day in her favorite pair of pastel ears and Robin wore a matching pair in Toronto.

"We got teased just like I expected," she told Theo. "But surprisingly not more than usual. And my art teacher ended up really digging the ears. She asked me where I got them so she could buy a pair."

That was the day Libby's outlook on life started to change – all thanks to a fearless friend and a pair of silly cat ears that still sat on top of her dresser at home.

"What about you?" she asked Theo. "What's the craziest thing you ever wore to the battleground that is high school?"

"Oh boy," Theo said. "Not cat ears, that's for sure. I wore a three-piece suit to my senior prom, though, and nearly passed out from nerves about how everybody was going to react. I was pretty much the only girl in the whole class who wasn't wearing a floor-length ball gown."

"And how did it go?"

"People said I looked good. I *did* look good," Theo said with a grin. "Haven't worn a dress since."

"Good for you," Libby said. "Wear what makes you happy." Her phone started to trill on the counter beside the computer. "Oh, damn, is it ten o'clock already?"

She reached across the counter to turn off her alarm and Theo said, "We've been talking for almost an hour. I'm sorry I took up all your time. You probably had work to do this morning."

Libby smiled. "I was just trying to figure some business-y things out. I wouldn't trade our conversation for all the strategic plans in the world."

"That does sound kind of dry," Theo agreed. "But it's up my alley, actually. I do social media marketing for small businesses and I can't even count the number of conference calls I've sat in on about inventory planning, marketing, budgeting, all that good stuff."

"You're making me dizzy," Libby teased. She really should have resisted the temptation to spend this hour with Theo – she was no closer to understanding the business side of Good Vibes, but she *was* a little more aware of how far over her head she was.

She unlocked the door and flipped the *Open* sign, then Theo drained the last of her coffee and handed Libby the empty mug. "Maybe I can help. What are you trying to learn?"

"Everything."

A couple of customers came in and Libby greeted them, then Theo took a flyer for an erotic massage workshop off the counter and turned it over, scribbling her number in the corner of the page. "Give me a call sometime. I've never worked with a boutique sex shop before, but business is business – I'll tell you what I can."

"I can't afford to hire you," Libby said. "I'm running a really tight ship as it is and things are about to get a whole lot tighter."

"Don't worry about it," Theo said.

She handed the flyer to Libby, who couldn't help teasing her. She'd gotten the girl's number after all. "So the way to your heart is through business?"

"Let's just call this making amends for a mistake yesterday," Theo said.

"Excuse me," a woman hauling a reluctant-looking spouse by the arm said as she approached the counter. "Do you have any costumes for beginner furries? We were thinking about a tail to start with."

Theo blushed. "I'll get out of your hair. Have a good day, Libby."

"Thanks," she said, lingering for an indulgent second on those great lips. Then Theo headed for the door and Libby turned her attention to the day's first customers. "Okay, let's talk tails!"

5

THEO

Tragically, all the booby balloons had deflated by the time Libby came over to the apartment to talk 'business-y things' with Theo the following Thursday evening.

Theo had chosen the date strategically, not on account of the booby balloons but because Andie had a weekly spin class that she never missed and that meant the apartment would be empty. When Theo told her she'd invited Libby over, Andie had practically tripped over herself to make plans to get drinks with a friend after class.

"I can't believe you asked her out," Andie said. "Well, not *out,* but still."

"And I can't believe you risked somebody swiping your phone just to force me to see her again."

"Worth it," Andie said with a self-satisfied smirk. "Besides, it's time for a phone upgrade anyway."

"But all those Nat Butler pictures-"

"Safe in the cloud," Andie said. "And in my heart." Theo made a gagging sound, then Andie gathered up her gym bag and water bottle and headed out the door with a lyrical, "Have fun!"

Libby arrived twenty minutes later – just long enough for Theo to work up a minor sweat doing last-minute tidying. She'd just changed into a fresh white t-shirt when the apartment buzzer sounded and her heart leaped into her throat.

It was silly to be worked up about Libby's visit. When Theo called to invite her over, she'd been as professional about it as possible just to make sure Libby had no delusions that this was anything other than a friendly business lesson. Libby was gorgeous and exciting and interesting, and it was true that Theo had spent more than one boring conference call during the last week staring into space and thinking about the faintly citrus smell she'd noticed whenever Libby came into her orbit.

But Theo didn't date because there was no way a girl like Libby would be happy to spend every night of her life on the couch. They were better off establishing a strictly friendly relationship from the outset.

Theo forced every butterfly in her stomach to vanish, then she cleared her throat and pushed the intercom button. "Hey, Libby. Come on up – third floor, apartment 302."

"Be there in a jiffy," Libby said as Theo buzzed her up. Even her voice had an energizing quality about it.

Theo opened the apartment door, then went into the kitchen to double-check the drink selection she'd asked

Andie to pick up on her last trip to the grocery store. Bottled water, soda, juice – all the usual stuff – plus a few more exotic choices because Libby seemed like an exotic kind of girl. There was kombucha, a six-pack of assorted craft beers, and another six-pack of organic iced teas just in case Libby didn't drink.

"Hello?"

Theo pulled her head out of the fridge. "Hi, come on in." Libby found her way to the kitchen and when she saw her, Theo let out an involuntary, "Wow."

"Do you like it?" Libby asked. She put her hand to her hair, now a vibrant purple styled into big, bouncy curls. "I just got it done yesterday."

"It looks great. Purple suits you."

"I was hoping you'd think so." Libby gave Theo a flirtatious smile – so much for setting a business tone for their meeting.

"Want something to drink?" Theo asked. "I've got lots of options."

She was just preparing to rattle off all the different varieties and flavors of drinks when Libby came over and opened the fridge to look for herself. Her hip touched Theo's and while she scanned the shelves, Libby asked, "No roommate tonight?"

"She's at spin class," Theo said. Grapefruit – that was the type of citrus Libby smelled like and God, was it intoxicating. "She'll be gone for hours."

"Good to know," Libby said. "I think I'll try the rhubarb ale. What are you drinking?"

"I had a honey weiss lager after work. I think I'll go

with the berry weiss next." Libby handed Theo's choice to her and she popped the caps off both bottles, then led Libby into the living room. "I brought my laptop out here if you want to work at the dining table, or we can sit on the couch."

"Couch sounds good."

Of course it did.

Theo pointed Libby toward it and followed behind her. Libby's purple locks bounced with each step and enticed Theo to look lower. The girl had great curves, accentuated by a tight, midriff-revealing top and a pair of floral-print jeans that looked like they were painted on.

Theo grabbed her laptop from the table and met Libby at the couch. The way she wrapped her lips around the mouth of her beer bottle was damn near obscene and Theo enjoyed the curve of Libby's neck as she tilted her head back to take a sip. If Theo had been the type of person who went for one-night stands, she'd probably have Libby pinned against the couch by now, exploring every inch of exposed skin with her mouth.

Instead, Theo set her laptop on the coffee table and passed Libby a coaster. "So, tell me more about your quest for 'business-y knowledge.' What are you hoping to achieve?"

"Financial independence," Libby said with a laugh. "My mom's been helping me run the store since I opened it and she's much better with the books and all that numbers stuff than I am. She's saved my butt a few times when sales weren't high enough to cover things like, oh, keeping the lights on. She's been a godsend but she's retiring next year, which means I'm going to be on my own financially."

"Does she work for you?"

"No, she's a sex therapist," Libby said. "She teaches workshops at Good Vibes, but mostly she offers moral and occasionally financial support."

"So you need to know where you stand and come up with a strategy to keep the lights on after she retires?" Theo asked.

"Exactly."

"Well, you're in luck," Theo said, opening her laptop. "Strategizing just so happens to be one of my specialties."

They settled into the couch, Theo with her laptop on her knees and Libby sitting shoulder-to-shoulder with her to look at the screen. Theo's work had more to do with social media presence, branding and engagement, but she remembered a thing or two from business school that would be useful for Libby. She pulled up an example of a strategic plan that she'd gotten on the Internet and explained the basic concept, then Libby rattled off half a dozen different strategic ideas she had for her business.

"We've got that erotic massage workshop next month," she said, ticking each idea off on her fingers while Theo mapped them all out on a quarterly planning calendar. "My mom teaches a monthly class on Tantric intimacy-"

"That sounds mortifying."

Libby laughed. "She's actually a really good teacher. That being said, I don't often attend her classes."

"Understandable."

"Oh, and I'm giving a talk on the empowering qualities of masturbation at SexyCon in September," Libby said. Theo was mid-sip and she nearly spit her beer all over her laptop.

"SexyCon?"

"Yeah," Libby said, turning to look at Theo. Her polished stone eyes were animated and it brought an involuntary smile to Theo's lips. "It's really cool – sex-positive workshops and lectures from people in all different industries, a huge vendor hall full of everything you can imagine, and a bunch of different play events. It's like a giant playground for adults."

"Very adult," Theo teased.

"You should check it out. I've gone every year since college and it's a blast," Libby said. "This is the first year I get to present, though."

"Well, it sounds like you've got a lot of good stuff going on for your business," Theo said, looking at the calendar she'd made. "I thought you were going to say you didn't have any promo plans."

"This is the big-picture stuff that I'm great at," Libby said. "It's filling out purchase orders and figuring out how much inventory I need that's a struggle – the little details that add up to be, apparently, pretty important."

"If you don't have good inventory control you can't very well meet your sales goals," Theo agreed.

Libby nodded eagerly. "That right there – I have no idea what any of those words meant. If I didn't have my mom and Josie to handle the day-to-day, I'd be completely sunk."

Theo laughed. "Okay, let's start with inventory control."

They spent the next half-hour building Libby's business vocabulary and when she reached the bottom of her rhubarb ale, Libby threw her arms out in a wide stretch. "What do you say we take a little break?"

"Sure."

Libby stood up, then reached for Theo's hand. "Wanna give me an apartment tour?"

She pulled Theo to her feet and they went back to the kitchen for a couple more beers, then Theo showed her around. It was a typical small New York apartment so there wasn't much to see.

"It's pretty much all visible from the couch," she explained.

"What about your room?"

"Down the hall," Theo said, pointing to a short hallway beside the TV stand. "Do you want to see it?"

"Yes, please."

Theo licked her lips, the butterflies making a reappearance. The sensation was not dissimilar to the one that consumed her when she strayed too far from safe spaces – an unsettled feeling in her stomach accompanied by a buzzing, electric feeling in her limbs.

Only this type of anxiety was pleasant, anticipatory – something Theo wanted to lean into – whereas she'd do almost anything to avoid the other kind.

Libby took Theo's hand and it sent a satisfying shiver through her. She walked a little faster toward the bedroom.

"Here it is," she said as she led Libby to the middle of the room. It was small like the rest of the apartment, and it felt even more cave-like thanks to the shelves that Theo had lined up against one wall to contain her game collection.

"Wow." Libby dropped Theo's hand and went to the shelves. "This has to be every card game ever invented."

"Nah, there are only a couple hundred here," Theo said. "Official estimates put the total number somewhere between a thousand and ten thousand."

"That's a big range," Libby said. "Who's 'official'?"

"The International Playing Card Society, of course."

Libby snorted, then turned back to the shelves, scanning them. "You can't possibly play all of these games. What do you do with them?"

"They're mostly for display," Theo said. "I like to study them, figure out the gameplay and strategy, and then they go up on the wall. Right now I'm getting to know all the expansion packs in *Escape from Moon Base 9*. Ever play it?"

Libby shook her head. "Maybe we can play together sometime."

She bit her lip, her words more innuendo than anything else. Theo found it so distracting that she barely even noticed herself blurting, "I figure all that research will come in handy if I ever want to create a game of my own."

"Oh yeah?" Libby asked, eyebrows rising with intrigue. "You want to be a game designer?"

"It's just a pipe dream," Theo backtracked. Why did she say that out loud?

"I've never known anyone who wanted to design card games," Libby said. "It's so retro." She gave the shelves one more glance and added, "This kind of reminds me of the Vibe Wall, actually. Have you played all of these?"

"Yep," Theo confirmed. "Although I'd hazard a guess that the practical experience of my hobby is a bit different from you experimenting with the items on your Vibe Wall."

"You don't get off on playing *Cards Against Humanity*?" Libby asked. Theo snorted and shook her head, so Libby shrugged. "Then I'm sorry, but my wall is clearly the superior one."

"You are the most honest person I've ever met," Theo said. "It's a little intimidating."

"My mom says it's an asset *and* a character flaw," Libby answered. "I just say what I'm thinking."

"That's pretty rare."

"Wouldn't you rather know where you stand with people instead of playing games?" Libby glanced at the wall again and smirked. "Or maybe you *do* like playing games."

"Not the mind game kind."

"Okay, then," Libby said, walking back to Theo with a sultry sway of her hips. She didn't stop until they were nearly chest-to-chest, then she looked up at Theo with unbridled desire in her eyes. "I like you, Theo. I think you're very sexy and you've got an intriguing air of mystery that makes me want to figure out what makes you tick."

Her tongue peeked out of her mouth, running slowly along her lower lip and leaving it glistening, inviting. When she reached up and threaded her fingers through Theo's short, wavy hair, Theo didn't stop her from bringing her head down to meet her. Libby was about four inches shorter than Theo and she rose onto her tiptoes to kiss Theo.

She tasted like vanilla and Theo inhaled her grapefruit scent deeply, filling her lungs with it. The butterflies were back in full force and Libby wrapped her arms around Theo's waist, pulling their bodies together. She was soft and her curves pressed against Theo in a way that made her ache for more.

When was the last time she'd felt another woman's body this intimately against her own? The cabin in the Catskills, three years ago...

Theo was beginning to forget how incredible it felt to mold herself to another person, to allow them to overwhelm every one of her senses and overtake her. To throw reason and sensibility aside and simply be.

But there was a reason for that.

She peeled herself away from Libby. She was still breathing heavy, her heart still pounding for her, when she cleared her throat and said, "Well, we better get back to work. That strategic plan isn't going to complete itself."

"Yeah," Libby agreed. She sounded disappointed, but she followed Theo back to the couch. "Did I overstep the boundaries?"

"No," Theo lied. "It's okay."

While Theo busied herself with the laptop, logging back in and figuring out where they'd left off, Libby took a long swig of beer, then surprised her. "Hey, there's this museum exhibition in town right now that I've been dying to go to. Would you want to go with me next weekend? As friends, of course."

Theo's pulse jumped again – *I'll take what's behind Anxiety Door Number Two* – but she could still taste the vanilla on her lips. She knew it was the wrong answer, that it would only lead to more panic attacks and disappointment all around, but she wanted more of that taste, more of Libby. So before she could talk herself out of it, she said, "Okay. But I'll meet you there."

Libby brightened. "No problem."

6

LIBBY

"Hey there, hot lips," Libby called when she spotted Theo coming up the sidewalk toward the museum. Theo looked self-consciously at the other people on the street but none of them were paying any attention – the benefit *and* the detriment of living in New York.

Unless your hair was on fire, nobody cared what you did.

"Hi," she said, offering Libby her elbow when they met. "You look beautiful."

"Oh, this old thing?" Libby said, twisting her hips a little so her skirt flared. She was wearing a short pinafore-style dress she'd sewn from yellow plaid, with vintage lace bloomers peeking out beneath it. "I got it from the thrift store – or at least, I got the components from the thrift store and reimagined them."

"You sew?"

"Here and there."

Theo smiled. "You're full of surprises."

"So are you," Libby said. She looped her arm in Theo's, brushing her hand over her crisp, blue collared shirt, and led her toward the museum entrance. "I figured you wouldn't want to come to the museum."

She and Theo had been texting since last Thursday. Libby had managed to learn a few more business terms for the mental glossary she was building and she'd also learned that Theo had a way of bringing a smile to her lips even in a text message. Libby was glued to her phone all week, hoping to see Theo's name every time a notification chimed, and lighting up every time it turned out to be her.

But she was also tempering her expectations for their museum date. Theo herself had a part in that, asking Libby a dozen probing questions about the museum, the exhibition, how long it would take to walk through it.

Well, you don't exactly walk through a Walther exhibition, she'd texted back. *But we can leave whenever you want.*

That seemed to help, but Theo's uneasiness was palpable and Libby kept expecting a cancellation text right up to the moment she saw Theo coming toward her on the sidewalk.

"What can I say? You made a compelling argument," she said as they paid admission and went inside.

"I can be persuasive," Libby agreed. She took Theo's hand and led her through the lobby. The Walther exhibition was in a special gallery and there were a few other museum patrons meandering toward it. Libby squeezed Theo's hand. "I'm glad you're here. I've been trying to get my mom to come with me to this for weeks. I've read a lot about the artist but I've never gotten to see any of his exhibitions."

"Is your mom going to be upset you went without her?"

"Nah," Libby said. "Especially not after I tell her I brought a date."

Theo's mouth narrowed into a slim line. Was that a misstep? Libby thought after their kiss that Theo was softening to the idea, but maybe she'd been wrong. She pushed open the gallery door and changed the subject.

"What should we do first?"

The gallery was one big room with white walls and polished wood floors. There were big swaths of variously shaped and colored fabrics arranged around the room in different configurations and the whole thing brought to mind a gymnastics competition. Only instead of gymnasts tumbling and twirling, there were grown New Yorkers uncertainly navigating the room, figuring out how to interact with each of the pieces.

"Whatever you want," Theo said. "I'm just along for the ride."

She smiled but it didn't quite reach her eyes. She seemed willing enough, though, so Libby pulled her over to a long band of gray cloth on the floor. Theo gave Libby a curious look.

"What do we do with it?"

"Put it on." A museum attendant appeared out of

nowhere, an older woman with a warm, encouraging smile. "Don't be shy."

Libby picked up one end of the cloth and the woman showed her how to wear the piece, like a hood that just so happened to be ten feet long. Theo donned the other half and asked, "Now what?"

"This piece is called the Sight Channel," the attendant said. "It's your own private world – an experience for two."

Libby felt the woman's hands on her shoulders, slowly guiding her backward until she reached the limits of the fabric and there Theo was, staring back at her from the other end. The attendant's hands disappeared and Libby smiled at Theo. "What do you think?"

"It's not the weirdest thing I've ever done with my head," Theo said. In the semi-darkness, Libby could just make out a smirk on her lips and suddenly the distance between them didn't feel quite so long.

Then Theo took off the Sight Channel and Libby rejoined her in the real world, blinking in the harshness of the overhead gallery lights.

"What should we do next?" Theo asked. She was looking around, not really seeing much. "Looks like that... umm, yoga mat?... is available."

Libby laughed. They went to a long red cloth at the other end of the room. Libby would have said 'floor runner,' but she could see where Theo was getting the yoga mat vibe. Libby brushed her hand over Theo's arm. "Are you having a good time?"

"Yeah."

"That wasn't very convincing."

"I'm sorry," Theo said. "What about you? Having fun?"

"I am." Interactive art wasn't for everyone and Libby couldn't fault Theo if Franz Erhard Walther failed to resonate with her, but it seemed like more than a bad art connection. So they explored the yoga mat – Action Path, according to the museum attendant – and watched another group navigate a wide white band of fabric, using their bodies as the structure that held it together. Then Libby said, "Let's get out of here."

Theo frowned. "Did I ruin this for you?"

"Not at all," Libby said. "I just wanted to play a little bit and I accomplished that. Did you hate it?"

"No."

"You can be honest."

"I really didn't."

"Was it me?" Libby couldn't bring herself to look at Theo when she asked. She just headed for the door, quickening her pace a little bit. She was generally good at reading people and she thought by the texts she and Theo had been sending all week that she was into her, despite her assertion that she didn't date. She'd been flirty enough, and she'd leaned into that kiss.

Now, Libby wasn't so sure.

"No," Theo said, adamant. "You're fantastic."

Libby stopped on the sidewalk, unable to keep herself from pouting slightly. "I don't feel fantastic. What changed?"

"The setting," Theo said. "I'm sorry. I really wanted

to just be normal for a night, but I was having a panic attack the entire time we were in there."

Libby's mouth dropped open. "What? Why didn't you say something?"

"And ruin our date?"

"I had no idea," she said. "You seemed fine. A little quiet, disengaged, but-"

"That's usually all it is, at least from the outside," Theo said. She wasn't meeting Libby's eyes – instead, she was intensely studying a crack in the sidewalk.

Libby took her hand. "I didn't know. I thought you were having a good time with me."

"I was," Theo said. "I am. It's a paradox, I know, and I won't blame you if you want to just call this whole experiment a failure and lose my number."

"How are you feeling right now?"

"Better now that we're outside."

"Well, it's a nice night," Libby said. "Do you want to go for a walk with me? If you're feeling up to it, I'd love to hear more about how you're feeling because I've got to confess, I don't understand."

"It's a puzzler," Theo agreed. "Let's walk."

They strolled hand-in-hand up the sidewalk. Libby aimed loosely for a public park she knew of about a half-dozen blocks from the museum and while they walked, she said, "So you can look completely calm on the outside and be having a panic attack on the inside. I always thought a panic attack was hysterics and breathing into a paper bag and all that."

"It can be," Theo said. "For me, the fear itself is losing

control – the hysterics, the hyperventilation. Sometimes, panic attacks can be completely invisible to the outside observer."

"What does it feel like?"

Theo didn't answer for a long time. They walked almost a block and Libby wondered if she was ignoring the question. Then, finally, she said, "It feels like being the main character in a horror movie, only nobody around you has gotten the message and you're the only one who knows the monsters are coming. You want to run or scream. Your whole body is on high alert, waiting for the danger, but everybody else is just going about their business, wondering what the heck your problem is."

Libby took a minute to respond, too. She tried to put herself in Theo's shoes, to feel what she'd apparently been feeling the whole time they were inside the museum. "Can you take medication to make the monsters go away?"

"I try not to unless I absolutely must," Theo said. "The panic goes away, but so does everything else. Every pill I've been prescribed just makes me extremely sleepy."

"Therapy?"

"Been there, done that, got the t-shirt," Theo joked. "It helps, but my insurance will only cover so many sessions each year so I try to ration them. I'm sorry we had to leave the museum after such a short time."

"I don't mind – my primary goal for tonight was to get to know you better and we're doing that now," Libby said.

She stopped short and gave Theo's hand a quick kiss. Then they turned into the park, lit from above by a canopy of string lights. "Besides, I think Franz Erhard Walther would have found a certain eloquence in it."

"How do you mean?"

"You went to his exhibition to interact with the environment in a novel way," she said. "It might not have been pleasant, but he *did* make you feel something."

"What did *you* feel?"

"Excited. Nervous. Curious," Libby said. "Amused. Did you see the couple asleep in the sleeping bags in the center of the room?"

"I must have missed that," Theo confessed.

"They were *really* getting into the exhibit."

"That or they found a really clever solution to the ever-rising New York housing costs," Theo suggested.

Libby laughed – there was the charming woman she'd been getting to know, emerging from the panic. She'd just needed a little air and some patience. Libby swung Theo's hand in an exaggerated arc as they followed the path that wound through the little park, listening to crickets chirp out their evening song.

They found a hot dog cart at the other end of the park and Theo treated Libby, then they sat down at a bench to eat. Libby tucked a napkin into her collar to protect her dress and Theo said, "So you're a seamstress. Was that a hard skill to pick up?"

"At first," Libby said. She snorted, dabbed a little mustard from the corner of her mouth and said, "The first thing I ever sewed was a Halloween costume with my mom. I was ten, completely obsessed with Victorian English fashion and drooling over this really expensive dress I found in a costume catalog. My dad had just left-"

"I'm sorry."

"Thanks. And there was no way my mom could afford to buy the dress in the catalog," Libby said. "But she could see how much it meant to me so she bought a bunch of discount fabric and the closest pattern she could find, and we brought my grandma's old sewing machine down from the attic. Neither of us had ever sewn a stitch before that."

"How did it go?"

"Disastrously," Libby said. "We started at the beginning of September and by Halloween I think we were both frustrated enough to settle for just sending me out there as a Victorian ghost or something. The sewing machine jammed all the time, the pattern was *way* harder to read than we expected, and the tulle to make the petticoat was not easy to work with. The dress looked like crap but we were proud of that stupid thing."

"Do you still have it?"

"It's at my mom's house somewhere," Libby said. "A monument to trying. My mom found a free sewing class at a local craft store that winter and enrolled me. It got a lot easier after that and I've been sewing ever since."

"That's impressive." Theo bridged the small gap on the bench between them, running one finger along the hem of Libby's dress. If not for the bloomers, she would have grazed her thigh and Libby craved the touch. Theo added, "I couldn't sew a straight line if you paid me, let alone have the imagination to create something that I didn't find on a clothing rack."

"I refuse to believe you have such a limited imagination. Sometimes you want something that just doesn't exist yet," Libby said. "You must understand that, otherwise you wouldn't have an entire wall of card games for research purposes."

"Yeah, but that's all it is – a wall," Theo said. "You actually go out there and make what you want, do what you want, get what you want. I'm sort of in awe of you, Libby."

"Sort of?"

"Okay, I am."

"I *do* get what I want," Libby said, leaning across the bench. She grabbed Theo by the collar of her shirt and kissed her hard. "How do you feel about coming back to my place for a nightcap? It's not far away and you can escape whenever you want."

She pulled back, looking into Theo's eyes, the color of a clear pond on a warm summer day. "I'd love to."

7
THEO

Theo crept into the apartment that night a little after midnight, closing the door quietly so as not to wake Andie... which would have been considerate if Andie wasn't waiting up for her on the couch.

The TV was on, muted with the picture casting shadows on the wall behind the couch. The moment Theo closed the door, Andie sat up with a grunt. She wiped the sleep from her eyes and asked, "What time is it?"

"Past your bedtime, apparently."

But Andie didn't need much in the way of a wake-up call. She was up and perky again, asking, "So, how did it go? It's late so that's a good sign, right? Or is it bad because you're home and not spending the night at her place?"

"Whoa. Calm down with the twenty questions."

Andie frowned and waited. Theo flopped on the couch beside her.

"I'm pretty sure it went well."

"Pretty sure?" Another frown.

"I had fun," Theo said. "The museum exhibition was bizarre and I had a panic attack, but Libby was really understanding about it."

More than Theo probably would have been if the tables had been turned.

"And?"

"And what?"

"And the museum isn't open until midnight, is it?"

"We went back to her place for a while," Theo said. Andie just stared at her – a look that demanded details – but Theo shook her head. "I don't kiss and tell."

"But there *was* kissing?"

A smile broke across Theo's face. "There was."

Libby was a fantastic kisser. Her body felt so *right* beneath Theo's hands and she couldn't get enough of that vanilla-mixed-with-grapefruit scent that was uniquely Libby. Every time Theo got within a couple feet of her, she wanted to circle Libby in her arms and devour her... and that was exactly why she'd politely extracted herself from Libby's couch a little before midnight and ended their date.

Theo hadn't felt that way in a long, long time. She couldn't recall *ever* feeling so strongly about a woman – even Dana, her one and only serious relationship. And Theo absolutely could not bear to fall in love with someone she knew her anxiety wouldn't allow her to have.

Libby was an adventurer. Theo could tell from the first moment she saw her that she craved experiences, novelty, excitement – the very things that sent Theo into a spiral of racing thoughts and nausea. Tonight had been fun. This whole week with her had been a blast. But could it be anything other than self-destructive to keep pursuing Libby?

"When are you seeing her next?" Andie asked.

Theo shrugged. "I don't know."

Her heart was pulling her in one direction, reminding her of all the things she'd spent the last three years pretending she didn't want – love, a partner, romance. Meanwhile, her nervous stomach was nagging her with all the reasons why she'd decided that stuff was too risky.

"Come on," Andie said, punching Theo in the arm.

"What the hell?"

"Don't be stupid," she said. "Anyone with eyes can see that you like her, and she's obviously good for you. She got you out of the house."

"I'm not that much of a hermit."

"You ordered toilet paper online last month rather than go to the store and buy it. *Toilet paper.*"

"It was a good deal," Theo defended herself. "And it's a pain in the ass hauling a jumbo pack of rolls around on the subway."

"I had to use paper towels to wipe for two days before it got here," Andie countered.

"Whatever, the paper towels were a good deal, too," Theo said. She crossed her arms but the longer Andie glared at her, the more she had to admit her roommate had a point. Theo wouldn't trek across town to the museum for just anybody, but Libby had made it worth the risk. Finally, she relented. "I was thinking about offering Libby more help with her business – some kind of weekly tutoring type of situation. She really is pretty lost."

Andie gave her a stern look. "It's a start. Okay, I'm going to bed. Love you."

"Love you, too," Theo said. She stretched out on the couch, unmuting the infomercial Andie had been watching, and let her mind wander back to the butterfly sensation in her stomach as Libby's lips brushed over hers.

Theo texted Libby the morning after their date and regretfully informed her that she was far too much of a chicken to wade back into the dating pool. She'd drafted at least a half-dozen texts trying to find the right words.

I had a great time but my anxiety monster did not.

I really like you but you also scare the shit out of me.

It's not you, it's the totally uninhibited way you live your life – I can't keep up.

Eventually, she'd settled on something a little less punchy and a little more honest. *I'm really enjoying getting to know you but I'm not ready to date. Can we take a step back and be friends?*

Theo's heart had stopped for the entire three minutes

that she stared at her phone and waited for Libby's response. If it had taken any longer, Theo might have died, but then those three little dots appeared, followed by Libby's response.

I'd love to be your friend.

Theo followed up by offering to take Libby on as a formal student and that made things a little easier. There was a structure to their strictly non-romantic relationship and it turned out to be mutually beneficial.

Libby was more than happy to accept Theo's one-on-one lessons, and she started to make some steady progress on her quest to save Good Vibes from her own ignorance. Meanwhile, Theo made a commitment to meet Libby once a week at the shop and it got her out of the house.

They picked Wednesday nights, which had the slowest customer traffic of the week, and Theo promised to come as soon as her work for the day was done.

The first time they met, Theo's heart was in her throat and her stomach was doing all sorts of unhappy flops the whole time while her mind demanded, over and over, to know *exactly* how long this was going to take and when she could get back to the safety of her apartment.

The second Wednesday, Libby had a pizza waiting but Theo was too nervous to eat it.

By the third week, she had become accustomed enough to the rhythm of customers coming and going, the sounds and smells of the shop – and the clearly-marked exits. She even managed to eat when Libby suggested they walk to the coffee shop next door and get a couple of bagels.

"We have to make it quick, though," Libby said. "I can't very well leave the store unattended."

"Hey, you're learning," Theo teased. "How did the erotic massage workshop go, by the way?"

"Very slippery," Libby said. "I had to make three passes with the mop to make sure nobody would wipe out while they were shopping the next day."

"And how did our lube table do?"

That was a question Theo never thought she'd ask, but she and Libby had come up with the idea to make sure her workshop attendees had the opportunity to also become customers. Rather than encouraging them to shop after the workshop, Libby and Josie set up a table full of massage-appropriate lubes along with the sign-in sheet, then made sure everyone walked past it again on their way out.

"I sold a bottle to almost every workshop attendee," Libby said. "And two of them came back later to buy other things. You're a marketing genius, Theo."

"I prefer 'marketing god'," Theo joked. "But no, that was all you. I just helped you figure out how to execute it."

"Let me buy your bagel, marketing god," Libby said. Theo tried to refuse but she insisted. "It's the least I can do in exchange for all your help."

They walked back down the sidewalk and Theo waited for Libby to unlock the shop door again. She caught a waft of grapefruit on the gentle evening wind and leaned into it. Libby had honored Theo's request for friendship but that didn't mean she'd stopped being completely intoxicating.

Theo closed her eyes until she heard the bell above the door jingle, then followed Libby back inside. They sat on twin stools at the counter while they ate their bagels and Libby chattered excitedly about SexyCon.

"I wish you could see it. If you think my Vibe Wall is nuts, you'd lose your mind in the vendor hall."

Theo laughed. "I just might go nuts. I don't do so well with big crowds."

"Maybe someday."

"Yeah," Theo agreed. It didn't hurt to daydream. "So, do you have your presentation all ready?"

"I'm going to wing it," Libby said, then laughed when she noticed Theo blanching.

"You don't have a speech? PowerPoint slides? Anything?"

"I've got talking points," Libby said with a shrug. "But I think the talk will come off sounding more genuine if it hasn't been rehearsed a thousand times."

Theo shook her head. "You really are fearless."

"I'm just passionate about what I do," Libby said. "Passion is all I need to speak from the heart."

"I don't know how you do it."

"What?"

"Get so excited," Theo said. "About everything. If I was giving a lecture, I'd have my speech written out word for word with stage directions and everything, and I'd be so nervous about the whole trip that I'd spend the whole time waiting for it to be over. I'm *already* doing that with my sister's bachelorette weekend. How do you do it?"

For the first time, Libby gave Theo a look that said she might be crazy after all. She blinked a few times, and her response was incredulous. "Well, I don't think that hard about it, for one thing."

"What do you mean?"

"You're so in your head all the time," Libby said. "It seems exhausting."

"It is."

"So why do you do it?"

"Because I'm not aware of any other options?" Theo said. "Are you telling me you never worry about that stuff?"

"I worry sometimes, sure," Libby said. "But I'd probably be agoraphobic too if I walked around thinking about every single step I had to take to get from one place to the next. I just do it."

"How very Nike of you."

Libby set her bagel down, wiped a bit of cream cheese from her fingers onto a napkin, then gave Theo a scrutinizing look.

"What?" Theo asked.

Then Libby leaned over and planted a kiss on Theo's lips. It reignited every single tiny flame in Theo's body that had begun to burn for her since the day they met, and she did it so casually.

She was back to her bagel before Theo's mind had even wrapped around what had happened, and Libby shrugged. "I just live in the moment. I let my heart lead me. I go on instinct. With the exception of strategic plans and balance sheets, it serves me pretty well."

Theo let out a long breath. She'd heard her therapist talk at length about the power of *living in the moment,* and every asshole with an anxiety podcast thought mindfulness was the answer to life, the universe and everything. But she'd never actually met someone who lived that way.

Libby seemed incapable of anything else.

What if it was just that simple? Just push away every scary thought, every worst-case scenario, every false alarm that her body sent to her brain to tell her the monsters were coming. And just be.

Theo was currently sharing a snack with a purple-haired beauty in a sex shop that, just a month ago, had nearly sent her into a full-blown panic attack simply for setting foot inside of it. Libby had motivated her to take a few steps outside her comfort zone for the first time since Dana broke up with her, and now that comfort zone was a little bit bigger. It stretched to include Good Vibes... and Libby herself.

Maybe there was more room for negotiation than Theo previously thought possible.

She slid off her stool, took a single step into Libby's personal space, wrapped her arms around her waist and kissed her hard. Libby let out a pleased little squeal and her body responded eagerly, tongue gliding out to dance with Theo's.

When the bell above the door jingled and a customer walked in, Theo released her, sat back down, and before she lost her nerve, she said, "Maybe I *will* see what SexyCon is all about."

"Really?" Libby's gorgeous, stony eyes were wide and sparkling.

Theo's stomach did a little flip.

8

LIBBY

Two weeks later, Libby was dragging her mom and Theo by the hand through a crowded parking lot in Philadelphia. She was wearing her colorful best – a patchwork skirt made up of all the band tees she'd worn threadbare and a jean jacket full of her favorite enamel pins. And she hadn't stopped talking since the three of them got in the car.

So much so that her mom periodically felt the need to remind her to breathe.

"This is going to be so much fun," she said as they approached a line of about twenty people at the door to the convention center. It was an unassuming, boxy building but Libby spent all year dreaming of what waited inside. "What should we do first? The vendor hall? Check out the exhibits? Go hear a talk?"

Her mom put her hand on Libby's shoulder and nodded subtly to Theo. *You're scaring the newbie.*

Theo did, in fact, have a somewhat wide-eyed expression on her face. That and the nervous energy vibrating through her palm and into Libby's were the only two indications of how she was feeling. If Libby wore her heart on her sleeve – literally, she was wearing an anatomical heart-shaped enamel pin in the colors of the pride rainbow – then Theo was a closed book.

She could be having a full-blown panic attack right now, like she had at the Walther exhibition, and Libby would have no idea. Libby had suggested Theo come for just a single day of the weekend-long SexyCon to dip her toe and see how she felt about it and that compromise seemed to set her more at ease, but Libby hated not being able to read her.

"How are you doing?"

"Good," Theo said, a thin smile painted across her lips. "How about we find a cup of coffee as our first order of business?"

"Sounds like a great idea," Libby's mom said with a yawn. They'd all been up before the sun but Libby wasn't feeling it at all.

The line advanced, they had their tickets scanned at the door, and a SexyCon volunteer gave Libby a lanyard with a 'Presenter' badge. She squealed as she put it on, pulled Theo and her mom in for a selfie, then turned with a flourish of her arms like she was Willy Wonka presenting the Chocolate Room.

"Welcome to SexyCon," she said, entirely for Theo's benefit because her mom came with her every year. "These are my people." Theo smiled and this time, it lit up those gorgeous, blue-gray eyes. Libby's chest gave an excited little flutter and she took Theo's hand again, kissing the back of her hand. "I'm so glad you're here."

They found their way to an alcove off the wide main hallway, where the convention center had set up a decadent breakfast buffet. There were lots of people milling around it and Libby weaved her way to a Danish and a cup of coffee.

"Oh my God, I love that pin," a girl with subtle green streaks in her hair said. She pointed out one of Libby's favorites – a wand massager with the words 'Self Love' inset in it that Robin had mailed to her when Libby had opened the shop. "Where did you get it?"

"It was a gift," Libby said. The girl pouted with envy and when Libby turned around, Theo was looking at her with one eyebrow raised. Libby laughed. "What?"

"You need to get your own pins made up for next year. Make them say Good Vibes instead and include your business card with each pin, then hand them out to anyone who wants one."

"That's a great idea," Libby's mom said, rejoining them with a couple cups of steaming hot coffee. She winked at Theo. "I like this one, Libby."

"Mo-oom." Libby did her best impersonation of a mortified teen, then linked her arm with Theo's. "I don't know the first thing about custom enamel pins but I guess I've got a year to figure it out."

"I'll help you," Theo offered. The blank, rigid expression she'd worn when they first arrived was disappearing by degrees and her body no longer stiffened against

Libby's touch. She hazarded a guess that Theo was enjoying herself.

They found a bar-height table to stand around while they drank their coffee and Libby's mom asked, "Are you ready for your big talk, sweetie?"

Libby checked her watch. "It's not for another three hours, but yes. I'm feeling good."

"Considering the subject of your talk, that's appropriate," Theo said.

Libby smirked. Theo was at a sex convention making masturbation jokes with Libby's mother within a few hours of meeting her – yeah, she'd fit right in with the Gromans if she ever quit fighting her own mind and admitted that she wanted to date instead of just stealing the odd kiss when the tension got too great.

"I'm excited for you," Libby's mom said. "You really got lucky, giving your talk the first year that the conference has a live streaming option – you'll be seen by thousands of people, not just the hundred or so in the room."

"Jeez, that's enough to give anyone stage fright," Theo said.

"Oh, not Libby." Her mom waved her hand at the idea. "My girl's not afraid of anything, are you, sweetie?"

Libby laughed. "Venomous snakes are pretty terrifying, and after our study session last week, I wouldn't want to meet a profit and loss sheet in a dark alley. But I love an audience."

She and Theo had talked extensively about the exposure opportunities Libby's SexyCon talk would present for Good Vibes. They'd mapped it on her shiny new strategic plan and marked it as a cornerstone event for the year. If Libby pitched her store well, everyone streaming SexyCon from New York City would come and check it out. Josie was optimistically manning the store, ready for the flood of new business.

"Enough shop talk," Libby said. "We've got a lot of time to kill before I need to get ready. Let's do some exploring!"

Libby led Theo and her mom through the crowded halls. They watched a veritable frenzy when a handful of big-name porn stars held an autograph signing session. There were acrobatic pole dancers and mesmerizing cage dancers throughout the large exhibit room. A drag contest was in progress on one of the stages.

And winding their way through all of it, there were the fans, the cosplayers, the fetishists, the shy observers – people of every orientation and sexual appetite free to be themselves if only for a single day, in this one special place.

In a word, it was heaven.

Libby was caught completely by surprise when, absorbed in a wax play demonstration, Theo nudged her and said, "It's eleven-thirty. Time to get ready for your talk."

"Already?"

"I can't wait to see you at that podium," Theo said. Libby pulled her in for a good luck kiss, then they found her mom watching a hypnotism act on one of the smaller stages and the three of them headed back up the hall.

The room where Libby was scheduled to give her talk was one of many that branched off the main hallway, a lecture going on in each of them. Libby left Theo and her mom to find chairs as her audience began to file in.

A SexyCon volunteer led her to the front of the room when they saw her 'Presenter' badge and outfitted her with a microphone. She powdered her nose and adjusted her clothes, then did a couple quick jumping jacks to shake out the fluttering sensation in her chest.

"You ready?" the volunteer asked.

Libby glanced over at Theo, who was looking back at her with awe, and at her mom, who looked proud before Libby had even said a word. The room was full, every chair taken, and a camera on a tripod sat in front of the podium, its recording light flashing. "Yes, I sure am."

The volunteer introduced Libby, then she took her place at the podium.

Deep breath. In, then out. Big smile.

"Hello, my name is Libby Groman and I'm here to talk about that dirty secret, masturbation." She got a few chuckles and a few uncomfortable looks from the audience. They all knew exactly what they were in for when they read the title of her talk on the sign outside the door, but Libby always had to warm people up to the subject of taking the self-guided tour. "But it doesn't deserve to be a dirty secret, does it? We all do it, even if some of us won't admit it even under threat of water torture. Hell, I did it this morning – who wouldn't want to start the day with an orgasm?"

Another few chuckles told her the audience was warming up and their energy began to vibrate through her. Libby was off to the races.

She stepped out from behind the podium, walking across the front of the room as she talked about the origins of her passion for sexual empowerment. "When I started my sex shop two years ago, I was inspired by my mother. She's right there – say hi, Mom."

Her mom shook her head, trying to refuse the attention, but in the end she had no choice but to turn and wave at the audience. Then Libby went on.

"My father left us when I was a freshman in high school. It was abrupt and even though she'd gone to college and studied psychology, my mom had spent the first fifteen years of my life as a housewife. When my dad left, we both had to adapt fast or perish, and my mom rose to the occasion. She learned how to be independent all over again. She refreshed her skills, got a day job to pay the bills and earned her Master's degree taking night classes. Then she took a huge leap of faith and started her own sex therapy practice. It was a difficult journey but she did it all with grace. I'm proud of you, Mom."

A small round of applause took over the room and Libby paused because her mom deserved every second of it. Theo was looking at her with a mix of surprise and admiration – Libby hadn't told her that story yet, and probably never would have volunteered the part about her dad leaving.

"That experience made my mother into a feminist, empowered to take care of herself and determined to instill those beliefs in me, too," Libby said. "That's why, when I talk to anyone who sets foot in my shop, I do so with a question in my head. How can I empower this person to love themselves, both literally and emotionally?"

That got another big round of applause. Libby grinned a little wider and turned, working her way back across the room in the other direction. The next forty-five minutes were a blur of positive vibes, applause, laughter and above all else, those blue-gray eyes glimmering proudly at Libby from the front row.

She could have gotten lost in them if she wasn't so hungry for the energy the whole room was showering on her.

At the bottom of the hour, just as Libby had the audience eating out of her hand, she saw the SexyCon volunteer walking over to the camera tripod, mouthing to her, *wrap it up.*

She had so much more to say. The whole talk felt like it had flown by in about five minutes even though her throat was parched and her underarms were sweaty from the overhead lights. Libby kept talking, pushing her time limit as far as she could because her audience loved her.

Wrap it up, the volunteer mouthed again, more insistent this time.

Libby looked at her mom and Theo, whose expressions had become frantic. Over what, she didn't know. Then Theo mouthed, *mention the shop.*

Oh, shit!

"Thank you so much for spending this time with me," Libby said, the sentence streaming out of her mouth as if it were one continuous word. "I'm Libby Groman and I'm the owner of Good Vibes sex shop." The volunteer was already walking away from the camera. The recording light no longer flashed. "Come visit us in the East Village in New York City."

She ended on a flat note even as the live audience gave her another very hearty round of applause. People started filing out of the room, ready to move on to their next adventure, and Libby slumped into a chair beside Theo.

"It didn't make it on the live stream," she said. "I got caught up in my talk and he stopped recording."

Theo put her hand on Libby's thigh, a cold comfort as the volunteer came and took away her microphone. Opportunity lost.

"Your talk was excellent, sweetie," her mom said.

"Thanks," Libby said, deflated. "Did I say the name of the shop at the beginning?"

She couldn't remember a word she'd said in the last hour but by the silence coming from Theo and her mom, she knew the answer was *no*.

"They know your name," Theo said. "They can still look you up and find the shop that way."

"The live stream audience doesn't even know what *state* it's in," Libby pointed out.

The three of them sat still for a few minutes while people moved around them. The next presenter arrived.

Her audience poured in and filled the seats around them, and Libby felt like sliding, spaghetti noodle limp, down to the matted red carpet.

The next talk began and the woman, wearing a structured blazer with her hair in a tidy ponytail, walked up to the podium and said, "My name is Denise Lawrence and I'm the owner of Slip & Slide, personal lubrication for every occasion."

Now that was a professional businesswoman who knew how to take an opportunity and run with it. Libby got up and made her way out of the room as non-disruptively as she could, not sticking around to find out how inclusive Slip & Slide really was.

By the time Theo and her mom followed her into the crowded hallway, she'd knocked the disappointment off her shoulders, lifted her head high and gave them a smile. "Do you think she really meant *every* occasion? What could you use Slip & Slide for at a wedding?"

"Favors?" Theo suggested.

9

THEO

There were at least two hundred people milling about in the wide hallway like blood cells through an artery. That would make Theo, Libby and her mom the plaque that was clogging the works.

The three of them stood outside the lecture room deciding on their next move. The people flowing around them made Theo dizzy and that old familiar feeling was rising again – the sensation of trying desperately to maintain control while everyone around her remained oblivious to the danger closing in. There were too many people, too few visible exits and far too many ways to get trapped – in the form of lecture rooms, exhibits, stages and vendor tables.

The only time the tides of panic had receded completely was when Libby was doing her thing during her presentation. Theo couldn't take her eyes off her.

Libby was entirely in her element, not only unafraid but drinking in the attention of her audience.

She was a port in the storm that had been raging in Theo's mind since they left New York, and she was undeniably amazing.

If only Theo had the words to tell her that. Right now, Libby was standing beside her with a plastic smile on her face, pretending Theo and her mother couldn't see how upset she was about the end of her talk.

"Who wants to attend a nipple play workshop with me?" she asked.

Libby's mom, Cora, laughed and bowed out. "I love you, sweetie, but we're not *that* close. Why don't you two do the workshop while I check out the Modern Feminism in Hollywood lecture that caught my eye?"

They agreed to meet up again near the snack buffet in a couple of hours, then Cora disappeared into the sea of people. When Theo and Libby were alone, Theo took her hand. "Are you okay?"

"Great," Libby said.

"Your talk was excellent." Theo tried to comfort her. "It was funny, smart, insightful... people will remember you for it even if you didn't get a chance to mention Good Vibes on the live stream."

Libby just smiled benignly, like she wasn't even hearing Theo. "It's all good – now let's have some real fun."

She dragged Theo into the sea and they rode the current into the exhibition hall that they'd taken a quick tour through prior to Libby's talk. There were stages at opposite ends of the massive room, performers weaving their way through the crowds, and the room was broken up with partition walls here and there to separate the various exhibits, workshops and play areas.

It was overwhelming.

"Wow," Theo said, trying to force a deep breath.

"Yeah, isn't it amazing?"

Then Libby was off again, expertly weaving through the crowds with Theo in tow. Libby got a few more compliments on her pins and her patchwork skirt, and soon the disappointment that had dampened her mood seemed to fall away.

"Thanks! I love your embroidered pasties!" she said to one woman, who gave her tassels a little twirl in response. A small surge of jealousy mixed with the anxiety in Theo's belly and she nudged Libby further into the crowd.

It was like a sexual circus, different acts going on everywhere Theo looked. They watched demonstrations of a lot of different toys and positions, Theo learned that soy candles were the safest beginner choice for wax play because they burned at the lowest temperature, and eventually she and Libby made their way to the nipple play workshop only to find that it was already in progress.

Theo and Libby stepped around a partition wall to find a group of about twenty people coupled up and playing with clamps, some giggling and others taking the lesson very seriously. The workshop leader was wandering among them, demonstrating the tools of the trade.

When she noticed the two late arrivals, she smiled warmly. "This session's full but I'm teaching again in an hour if you want to come back."

"Okay, thanks," Libby said. "Maybe we will."

A few people were brazenly removing their shirts to play with the clamps as Theo led Libby back to the exhibition hall. "I'm not sure I'm ready to step *that* far out of my comfort zone."

"No problem," Libby said, rising onto her tiptoes to give Theo a kiss on the cheek. "There's plenty to do here that doesn't involve getting naked in public."

"Thank God for that. I've never been the sexually adventurous type, but I'm willing to do anything here that's on the educational end of things."

"Ooh, there's a bondage demonstration," Libby said, pointing across the aisle. "Ever tried it?"

Get voluntarily tied down and submit to the whims of a partner? No, thank you. Theo shook her head and Libby's eyes lit up. She led the way and they joined a group of three watching as a woman with brilliant blue eyes tied different types of knots around the wrists and arms of her audience.

"Okay, let's move on to another basic tool in the dominant partner's repertoire – the handcuff knot," she said, looking around. "Can I have a volunteer?"

Her eyes settled on Libby and another wave of jealousy washed over Theo. She'd never seen so many half-naked people with their sexual predilections on display in her life and it was doing a number on not only her agoraphobia, but on the way she felt about Libby. All of a sudden, her insistence on keeping things casual and friendly was beginning to seem pretty questionable.

Libby liked her and Theo liked Libby back, but how long would she stick around playing this friendship game if Theo didn't make more of an effort to overcome her anxiety and her old emotional wounds?

"I'll do it," she found herself blurting, holding out her wrists.

Libby looked shocked, but she put her hand on Theo's lower back and gently pushed her forward. "I'm pleasantly surprised. Have fun."

Theo's heart was pounding as she approached the blue-eyed woman with a rope already in hand. The instant she'd volunteered, she started second-guessing herself. Why did she do that? And for a handcuff knot, of all things? Theo's stomach twisted and the room felt ten degrees hotter.

"This one's deceptively simple," the woman said, positioning Theo's hands like a jailer about to arrest her perpetrator. "You're going to start with two simple loops, then overlap them like so."

Theo glanced at Libby. Her whole body was boiling with fear but Libby just looked excited as always. Oh, to be carefree and actually enjoy the present moment... a task much easier said than done.

In a quick couple of steps, the woman had Theo's wrists encircled in the rope and the second she tugged them tight, the panic bubbled over.

"I changed my mind," Theo said. "Get me out of this."

The woman's mouth dropped open but she didn't move fast enough to loosen the rope. "Are you okay?"

"Theo-" Libby started to say.

"I have to go," Theo interrupted them both, yanking her wrists free. Her heart was in her throat, her stomach threatened to release its contents one way or another, and all she could think about was getting out of that goddamn convention center.

She left the rope on the floor, left Libby staring in open-mouthed horror, and bolted for the door. The volume of the crowd did nothing to calm her racing pulse. It was like swimming through mud trying to part them and all Theo could think was *get out, get out, GET OUT*.

That command blotted out the whole world – nothing else mattered.

By the time she reached the parking lot, she was gulping down fresh air, completely unconcerned with how she looked to the people around her. She took a pill out of her pants pocket and dry-swallowed it. She'd been hopeful this morning that she wouldn't need it – she hadn't had to take one in months – but she'd also been realistic enough to bring it just in case.

While she waited for the pill to take effect, Theo paced back and forth along the front of the building and her heart continued to race. On her third turn, she saw Libby coming out of the convention center.

"Hey," she said, approaching Theo like she was a frightened animal. "How are you doing?"

"I'm sorry."

"Don't apologize. I'm just worried about you."

Theo took another long, deep breath. She had to force the air into her lungs – the tendency was to hyperventilate, but all that did was make her dizzier and sicker. "I really tried to just be normal for a day. I didn't want to ruin your fun."

It felt a little better to be outside – far better than having that rope twisted around her wrists – but the fact remained that she was a two-hour drive away from the safe refuge of her apartment. And before they could leave, they'd have to go back inside and find Cora. And there'd be traffic on the way home, and-

"Hey," Libby snapped, loud enough to break through to Theo. "Where are you?"

"Huh?"

"You looked miles away."

"I feel sick. I don't know why I thought I could handle this."

"Come here," Libby said, taking her hand. "Let's sit down for a minute." She led Theo over to a bench along the wall and even though sitting was the last thing she wanted to do, Theo did. Libby ran her hand up and down over Theo's arm. "Take another deep breath. I'll do it with you."

Theo watched Libby's chest rise, rise, rise, then fall.

Theo breathed with her.

And again.

And again.

Slowly, between the breathing, the steady stroke of Libby's hand over Theo's arm, and the medication making its way into her bloodstream, Theo's pulse returned to normal. The sickness faded and her thoughts stopped screaming.

Libby sensed the change and wrapped her arms around Theo, pulling her head down to her chest. "Better?"

Theo nodded. She felt like hiding her face in the folds of Libby's skirt like a child hiding behind her mother. Now that she could think again, her mind insisted on replaying the whole episode in excruciating detail, showing her just how unhinged she'd been.

"I'm so embarrassed."

"Don't be," Libby said, running her fingers through Theo's short hair.

She must think less of Theo now – how could she *not* judge her when something as simple as a piece of rope had the power to completely undo her? "Did you think the bondage demonstrator was pretty?"

Libby turned Theo's chin up to look her in the eyes. "Is that what was bothering you?"

"That was part of it," Theo confessed. If she was going to have a full-blown panic attack in front of this fearless woman, she might as well be honest about it. "I felt trapped and I felt stupid for keeping you at arm's length."

"Well, she did have you cuffed," Libby pointed out. "But to answer your question, she's not my type. Even if she was, I hope you think better of me than to expect me to hit on someone else right in front of you. I like you, Theo."

"I do think better of you," Theo said. "And I like you, too."

She felt weak, exhausted in the wake of panic like she'd used up all the energy in her body, and the medication had stolen what was left. She didn't have the strength to explain how jealous she'd gotten inside the exhibit hall when she realized how badly she wanted Libby all to herself, or that she was still afraid of what would happen if they tried seriously dating, or that she'd been so overwhelmed by the chaos inside the convention center.

"I had to take an anti-anxiety pill," she said instead. "I'm going to be pretty lethargic for the rest of the day."

"That's okay," Libby said. "As long as you're feeling better. We'll take it easy. Do you want to stay out here or go back in?"

Theo sat up and took a deep breath. She did a mental scan of her body. As tired as those pills made her, they did manage to wipe out every trace of anxiety and made her as easy-going as she wished she could be without them. "Let's go back in. I'm okay now."

"Good." Libby pulled her to her feet. "We haven't even seen the vendor hall yet and they always have fun things in there. It's just tables and walking – no more bondage, I promise."

Libby looped her arm in Theo's and led her back inside. She floated through the vendor hall, trying to focus on the things Libby pointed out while the medication fog settled in her brain.

Cora found them about an hour later, three hot pretzels and sodas in hand. She told them about the lectures she'd attended and the orgasm control class she'd taken – which failed to register so much as an *oh, that's neat* reaction from Libby. If Theo's own mother had ever uttered the phrase 'orgasm control' in her presence, they would have both died instantly of mortification.

"We've been looking at the toys," Libby told her casually. "I think I'm going to order some pendant vibrators for the shop when we get home – jewelry that can make you come like a porn star is the wave of the future."

Cora passed around their afternoon snacks and thanks to the medication, even Theo had managed to work up an appetite. They meandered through the vendor hall while they ate and the pretzel perked Theo up a bit, drawing her out of her brain fog.

"Ooh, sex dice," Libby said, bumping Theo's hip and sending her in the direction of the table that drew her attention.

There were colorful, oversized dice spread all over the tablecloth and an eager couple waiting for their next customers. "Hello. Have you ever tried sex dice before?"

"Nope, but I'm willing to give it a whirl!" Libby picked up a pair and tossed them on the table. "Lick... neck. Don't mind if I do."

She cupped Theo's head in one hand and ran her tongue from her collar up to her jaw. Theo might have been doped to the gills, but she sure as hell felt that. As a shiver worked its way through her, a goofy smile came involuntarily to her lips.

"I think your girlfriend likes them," the female half of

the sex dice couple said. "You should bring home a set for further exploration."

Libby reached for her wallet but Theo impulsively took her hand to stop her. Libby frowned but Theo gave her a reassuring wink. "Libby is the owner of a female empowerment-focused sex shop in New York City. This is just the type of product her customers would love."

"What's the name of the shop?" the man behind the table asked.

"Good Vibes," Libby said.

"She just did a talk this morning," Theo said, pointing to Libby's Presenter badge. They really should have had business cards printed up before SexyCon. "It was very well-received."

"Why don't we give you a pair of dice on the house?" the woman said. "Try them out and see what you think. Our website's printed on the packaging when you're ready to place an order."

"Thanks," Libby said. She took the dice, then pulled Theo and her mom away from the table. "That was kind of morally ambiguous, wasn't it?"

"What?"

"Using my shop to get free stuff."

"It's not free stuff if you're genuinely interested in selling it," Theo said.

"They *would* be a good addition to the shop," Cora pointed out. "Sex games are very popular right now."

"They are?" Theo asked.

"I learned it in one of the lectures I attended."

"Okay," Libby said. "But now you have to help me test them, Theo."

"I can do that." Theo took the package from her, turning it over as they headed deeper into the vendor hall.

Sex games were popular, huh? There was a lightbulb trying to go off in Theo's head, shining its brightest to pierce through the medication fog.

10

LIBBY

It was late when they got back to New York and Theo had been so exhausted from her medication that Libby convinced her to crash at her place. And crash, she did – Theo was out like a light the moment her head hit the pillow.

She looked peaceful when she slept, all the tension she held in her body melting away as her chest gently rose and fell.

Libby tiptoed around the tiny apartment above her shop, washing off her makeup and putting her convention outfit in the laundry hamper. Theo had spent all her nervous energy at SexyCon, but Libby felt the first twinge of her own fearfulness when it was time to slide into bed beside her.

She was bare-faced, wearing an oversized t-shirt and gray cotton sleep pants, and she couldn't remember the last time she'd simply slept beside another woman.

It wasn't the sleeping that worried her. That was easy.

The hard part was facing the uncertainty of what awaited her when she woke up the next morning. Option number one, Theo silently let herself out of the apartment in the middle of the night and Libby woke up alone. Option number two, Libby snored or farted or drooled in her sleep and Theo decided she never wanted to spend another night like that again.

Option three, Libby awoke to find Theo still beside her, oblivious to any involuntary nighttime emissions her body made but thoroughly disillusioned to see Libby in her baggy sleep clothes, flaws hanging out all over the place.

Maybe she should have slept in her makeup.

When morning finally did come, Libby woke to a completely different set of insecurities.

You really screwed up yesterday.

That was her first thought as her eyes fluttered open. Apparently while her conscious mind was busy worrying about whether or not she drooled, her subconscious mind was still dwelling on that failed opportunity at SexyCon. Libby even had a vague sense that she'd been dreaming of delivering her talk naked while her audience laughed and pointed at her.

She groaned and rolled over to bury her face in the pillow, but bumped into Theo instead. Still there, still sleeping.

Libby inched away from her, intent on scurrying into the bathroom to put on a fresh face of makeup and some better clothes before Theo woke up. But she didn't make it far before Theo's arm circled her waist and pulled her back into bed.

"G'morning," she murmured, burying her face in Libby's neck and kissing her.

It felt nice, and with Theo's strong arms around her, Libby wasn't getting out of this easily. She'd just have to fake it as best she could. She put on a smile, then rolled over to face Theo. "Good morning, sleepyhead. Are you feeling refreshed?"

"Very. Thanks for letting me sleep here – I'm sure your mom would have had to drag me up to my apartment if I'd tried to make it all the way home."

"Is Andie going to be worried about you?"

"Nah," Theo said. "She's probably celebrating. She's been trying to push me out of my comfort zone for months... *years,* actually."

She let Libby go so she could throw her arms wide in a deep stretch. The bedroom was so small Theo's hands practically touched both walls and the morning sun was just beginning to stream through the window that served as Libby's headboard. She could hear the city sounds outside – cars and pedestrians and street carts with piping hot coffee all contributing to the chaos that she loved so much.

Libby propped herself up on one elbow and asked, "How does that work, exactly?"

"What?"

"Your comfort zone. It must be scary never knowing what's going to set off a panic attack," she said, finger-combing Theo's hair out of her eyes. "It looked like an awful thing to go through when you had one yesterday, but you seem okay this morning. Are you?"

"Yes," Theo said. "But I hate talking about this because when I say it out loud, it sounds like such a stupid problem to have – like I should be able to just *stop panicking.*"

"You don't have to talk about it if you don't want to."

"No, you've been really patient and I'd like to try to explain it," Theo said. She sat up and Libby did the same, tucking herself into the crook of Theo's arm. "It's all relative. If I never leave my apartment, I start to think of it as safe. I don't get sick, I don't have panic attacks, so it must be okay to be there. It was really hard to come here for our weekly meetings the first few times because it was a huge change, but it's starting to become another safe space for me."

"I'm glad. I love having you here."

"I wanted to go to SexyCon with you because I know how important your presentation was, and I wanted to be there to support you. But the whole event had me on edge because it was so far from home. I've never been to that convention center before and I had to rely on your mom to bring me back to a safe place," Theo said. She paused, looked down at her lap and added, "Yeah, this sounds so stupid and illogical."

"It *is* a little illogical," Libby admitted, "but it's not stupid. How could your feelings be stupid? They're how you experience the world."

Theo hugged her a little tighter. "Thank you. I wasn't always like this, you know."

"Oh?"

"My world used to be a lot bigger."

Libby waited because it seemed like Theo had more to say, but she didn't go on. In the end, Libby had to prompt her. "What happened?"

Theo was reluctant when she spoke again. "I had this girlfriend – it was pretty serious and she wanted to get married. All our friends expected us to. They kept saying how we looked like the perfect couple, but it just didn't feel right to me. She didn't feel like the person I was meant to spend my life with."

"So you broke up and retreated into your shell?" Libby guessed.

"The reverse, actually," Theo said. "I was too much of a coward to break up with her so I let my anxiety get the best of me. I let my world get smaller and smaller. I took a job working from home, I stopped going out with our friends, stopped taking her on dates. I didn't do any of it intentionally but deep down, I think I figured if I was a hermit, she wouldn't want to be with me anymore." She shrugged. "It worked."

"Congratulations?" Libby said.

"That was three years ago," Theo said. "I saw pictures of her wedding a few months ago – she got back together with an ex and she seems happy now. So it worked out for the best – at least for her."

Libby wrapped her arms around Theo and squeezed. "You don't have to settle for this, you know. You can make your world bigger again. First step, SexyCon, next step, the world." Theo's muscles tensed against her – too much, too fast?

"I meant what I said outside the convention center, you know," Theo said. "I really like you."

"And I meant what I said – I like you, too, Theo." Libby snuggled against her.

"I don't want to push you away, too," Theo said. "I've been trying to keep things between us platonic because I'm in no condition to date someone when I have panic attacks just trying to leave my apartment. I don't want to drag you down with me or ask you to make your world as small as mine. But it is *really* hard to keep myself from crossing lines when your curves are pressed up against me like this." She dipped her head and inhaled, then said, "You smell like grapefruit."

"It's my shampoo."

"It's intoxicating," she growled.

Libby felt a shiver of desire work its way through her, a strange mix of arousal and self-consciousness because she couldn't forget the fact that she was bare-faced and wearing nothing but a t-shirt and pajama shorts. Could Theo really want her even without any of her armor on?

She sat up to look her in the eyes. "I don't want you to worry about making my world smaller, or holding me back. If we like each other, then we owe it to ourselves to give it a try and see where this goes." She chuckled and added, "We've been doing a pretty shitty job of being platonic, anyway."

Theo smiled. "Okay. Let's give it a try."

Libby leaned over and kissed her, letting herself linger in the moment. When she pulled back, she said, "I really appreciated you going to the convention with me, by the way. I know how hard it was for you and it meant a lot to have you by my side, even if I did muck up the end of my talk."

"Your talk was amazing," Theo said. "You were radiant and you had everyone on the edge of their seats. Don't beat yourself up too much about the ending – there will be other opportunities."

"I won't if *you* promise not to beat yourself up about your agoraphobia," Libby said. "I guess we both have things to work on."

"I guess we do." Theo kissed the top of her head and Libby rested against her shoulder. Then Theo said, "I was sorry to hear about your dad leaving – I didn't know that. It must have been heartbreaking."

Libby's chest tightened. All she managed to say was, "Yeah, it wasn't fun." Then she crawled out of bed, pulling Theo to her feet and saying, "I think it's past time for a cup of coffee. Want one?"

Why was it so easy to open up to a room full of strangers, and yet when Theo asked about her dad, she would have rather taken her chances on the rusty, ancient fire escape outside her window?

"Sure," Theo said. "Did I say something wrong?"

"No. I just need my morning dose of caffeine."

Libby went into the small kitchen at the back of the apartment and busied herself with the coffee maker while Theo leaned against the counter nearby. She didn't push the subject of Libby's dad any further and Libby didn't offer any more details.

While the coffee percolated, Libby went over to the dining table and up-ended the tote bag full of convention swag they'd collected in the vendor hall. She and Theo sat down to sift through it all.

There were pins, pens, business cards and magnets from companies that had caught Libby's eye. She'd bought a suction-based oral sex simulator that she was looking forward to giving a test run for possible inclusion on the Vibe Wall, plus some silk bondage ropes that were too pretty to pass up, and there were the sex dice Theo had managed to score for free.

"You were really good with that vendor," Libby said, taking the dice out of the packaging. "I should bring you with me every year."

"I help clients with that sort of thing all the time," Theo said. "It's second-nature once you get used to it."

Libby tossed the dice. *Kiss. Hand.* "Well, that's an easy one."

She took Theo's hand and did as the dice commanded, then Theo rolled them. *Blow. Navel.* Libby laughed but Theo just shrugged. "The dice want me to give you raspberries."

"Don't," Libby giggled.

"It's the rules."

Theo grabbed her, pinning her to the chair while Libby struggled. She lifted her shirt and blew raspberries on Libby's belly, then planted a kiss on her lips for good measure. Still giggling, Libby got up to retrieve their coffee cups and Theo gave the dice another roll.

"You know, these things are giving me an idea," Theo said.

Libby came back and set Theo's coffee down, then looked at what she'd rolled. "An idea to lick my nipples?"

"I wouldn't object to that," Theo said. "But there's something else, too. Your mom said sex games are popular. What if I make my own, a sexy card game?"

"Really? What would the concept be?"

"I'm not sure yet," Theo said. "Do you think something like that would sell in your shop?"

"If you developed a game, I'd pimp it out to everyone who came within twenty feet of Good Vibes," Libby said, then winked. "But at a price."

"Which is?"

Libby nodded to the dice. *Lick. Nipples.*

"I thought you needed your morning caffeine," Theo pointed out.

"Well, now I need something different," Libby answered. She straddled Theo's lap, bowing her head to kiss her.

Theo slid her hands beneath Libby's t-shirt, cupping her palms over Libby's bare breasts. "You look sexy as hell in your jammies, by the way." Libby rolled her eyes so Theo pinched her nipples. "I'm serious. If I woke up to this view every morning, I'd have two reasons to never leave the house."

"Are you saying I'm bad for your recovery?"

"Quite the contrary." She finished the job of pulling

Libby's shirt over her head, then wrapped her arms tight around her and rolled her tongue slowly over one nipple, then the next.

Libby turned to putty in her embrace, rocking her hips forward as her body responded. When Theo looked up at her, those blue-gray eyes filled with desire, a shiver of fear ran through Libby. You had to be really vulnerable to look at somebody like that, and in that way, Theo had the upper hand.

"Your turn," Theo murmured. She grabbed the dice from the table and handed them to Libby.

There was *Bite Thigh.* Then *Touch Breast.* And *Kiss Earlobe.*

Theo's body felt firm and warm, and *right* against Libby's softer curves. Every time their lips met, it felt like coming home, being right where she should be at exactly the moment she needed to be there. And her whole body was responding to her, tingling with desire and anticipating every roll of the dice. Every touch of Theo's lips against her skin. Every movement.

It felt good to be with someone she'd come to care about, to explore a physical connection in the wake of an emotional one. Theo was so much more than just flirty looks and meaningless fun. Who knew it would feel better, too?

The game broke down a little when they got to *Blow Ass* and the mood was broken as they both devolved into a fit of giggles.

"No offense, but I'm not sure I'm ready to go there with you yet," Theo said.

"None taken," Libby said. "When you design your own game, make sure there are a minimum of mood killers."

"You'll just have to help me test it out to make sure."

"It would be my pleasure. Literally, if the game is any good."

Libby gave Theo another long kiss, then said, "So I was thinking, wouldn't it be fun to have a Halloween party at the shop? We could make it like a miniature version of the exhibition hall, with demonstrations and experiences for the guests, and everyone could wear the naughty costume of their choice."

Theo grinned.

"What?"

"Don't look now, but you're doing strategic planning."

Libby smirked at her. "Maybe you're rubbing off on me after all. So, would you be my date for the party?"

"Yes," Theo said. "I definitely would."

"Good. And we've got over a month to plan it," Libby said.

She gave the dice another roll – *Kiss Thigh* – then slid off the chair, spreading Theo's knees and settling between them.

11

THEO

October came and went in a blur of work shifts that all felt the same – conference calls and virtual client meetings and spreadsheets that mattered less to Theo with every passing day. She'd always approached her job with a sense of robotic duty. It was something to get through, a necessity that neither brought joy nor inspired her life.

Now, it was just eight long hours each day that kept her chained to her computer, separated from Libby.

The closer they got, the more Theo saw how incredible that girl was. Their weekly tutoring sessions turned into almost daily excuses to see each other, and even though they rarely strayed farther than their apartments, Libby didn't seem to mind the constraint.

She found restaurants to order take-out from. She volunteered to make the trek across town to Theo's place on days when her nerves were feeling particularly frayed. She came up with creative little dates that didn't involve leaving Theo's comfort zones, like picnicking on the fire escape and building a blanket fort like a couple of kids, then watching movies under it until they fell asleep in each other's arms.

One night toward the end of October, Theo stood in the narrow doorway to Libby's bathroom and watched her bleach and then dye her hair in a Harley Quinn two-tone style, blue on one side and pink on the other. They listened to an old Nat Butler album because Andie had turned Libby onto her, and Theo's heart felt full every time she caught Libby's gaze in the mirror.

She was amazing, patient, understanding and beautiful.

And she made Theo want to try harder.

That was why, on Halloween night, she showed up at Good Vibes in a full Joker costume, green hair and everything, with Andie and Penny in tow. Andie was a sexy pizza slice – something Theo was pretty sure violated the laws of man *and* nature – and Penny was in a form-fitting black dress with a mouse ear headband that seemed like a bit of an afterthought. Theo and Andie had teased her accordingly before they left the apartment.

"Do you even know how much a bridal bouquet costs?" Penny had retorted. "All my money's going into the wedding. At least I'm not fetishizing Italian cuisine."

"Bite me," Andie shot back with a smirk.

Penny ignored her, turning her attention to Theo. "Are you going to be okay tonight? It's probably going to be crowded."

"Don't psych her out," Andie said.

"I'll be fine. I've been to Good Vibes a hundred times."

She had an anti-anxiety pill tucked into her pocket just in case, but she hadn't needed one since SexyCon and she was determined not to break the streak tonight. She was going to be charming and fun, exactly the kind of easy-going girl she imagined Libby with because that was who she deserved.

Theo had to be worthy of her because she was thinking of asking Libby to be her girlfriend. It scared the hell out of her, but what else was new?

When the trio arrived around nine o'clock, the door to Good Vibes was propped open to encourage Halloween revelers to drop in on their way from bar to bar. It was a cold night, so Libby had put out a sidewalk sign to tempt people inside.

Come warm up with us – we'll stoke your fire!

The small shop was crowded with a mix of partiers and shoppers – and partying shoppers. Theo said hello to Josie behind the counter, then found Libby near the back of the store.

She was in the middle of an animated discussion with Cora and a chubby brunette in a unicorn onesie, so absorbed in their conversation that she didn't notice Theo's arrival.

She took the opportunity to drink Libby in. Her Harley Quinn dye job was up in pigtails just like Margot Robbie's and she had on a pair of hand-sewn blue and red shorts so small her round cheeks peeked out of them. She'd cut up a baseball tee, her breasts swelling from the low-cut neckline, and the soft skin of her stomach was bared, too.

Theo could hardly breathe by the time Libby turned and caught her eyes.

"*Damn*, you look hot," Theo growled, wrapping her arm around Libby's waist. "Please tell me you don't dress like this every Halloween."

Libby giggled. "It's a costume party at a sex shop. What did you expect?"

Theo pulled her in for a kiss, then whispered in her ear, "I'm not going to be able to keep my hands off you tonight."

"You'll have to try," Libby said. "At least for a few hours. Theo, you know my mom, of course-"

"Hi, Cora."

"Hi, sweetie." Cora was dressed conservatively, with cat ears on her head and whiskers painted onto her cheeks.

Theo introduced her to Andie and Penny, joking, "Looks like we've got a cat and a mouse tonight. Be nice to each other."

"Don't worry, I've had my claws trimmed," Cora said.

"And we just ate," Libby added. Then she put her arm around the chubby brunette, pushing her a few steps closer to Theo. Libby was beaming as she said, "Theo, this is Robin. She came in from Toronto just this morning."

Theo was momentarily without words. Robin, the girl who had brought Libby out of her shell when they were kids. The friend she'd come out with. The one she suspected, by the way she talked about her, had been Libby's first crush.

"The famous Robin," Theo said, standing a little taller as she held out her hand. "Nice to meet you."

"You, too." Robin took her hand, but her shake was brief and she didn't meet Theo's eyes.

"So you came all the way from Canada for Libby's Halloween party?"

"No," Robin said. "I'm attending a conference for work tomorrow in the city. I was going to come in the morning, but when Libby mentioned her party, I drove down early."

"We haven't seen each other in ages," Libby said, giving the girl a quick hug. "We like to get together about once a year, but I think the last time was Christmas. I'm so glad you two get to meet!"

Theo forced a smile. Robin was a lot prettier than she'd been picturing when Libby mentioned her, and more feminine, too. She couldn't think of a single thing to say to Libby's hopefully ex-crush. Thankfully, Andie was there to save her.

"Oh my gosh, I *love* that costume," she said, running one hand down the plush sleeve of Robin's onesie. "I bet you're so comfy and warm right now."

Oh, brother. Nobody could fall in love at first sight quite like Andie.

"Anyone want a drink?" Libby asked. "I'm not allowed to serve alcohol to the customers – no liquor license – but I've got a case of beer in the back for friends."

"I'll take one," Penny said, accompanied by a chorus of *me too* from the rest of the group.

"I'll come with you," Theo said, following Libby into the office behind the checkout counter. She closed the door behind her and the moment they were alone, she planted a fierce, possessive kiss on Libby's lips.

"What was that for?"

"I told you – you look hot as hell."

"So do you, Joker." Libby ran her hand down the front of Theo's garish green vest – she'd gone Heath Ledger rather than Jared Leto and now that she'd met Robin, she was glad she'd stopped at the hair and skipped the psychotic makeup.

"You don't like her, do you?"

"Huh?"

"Robin," Libby said. "She's really shy and sometimes people mistake it for arrogance."

"I don't dislike her," Theo said. "I just met her."

"Promise me you'll spend a little time getting to know her," Libby said. "She's been my best friend forever."

"Just your best friend?"

Libby pushed Theo up against the desk in the center of the room, their hips connecting and sending pleasure coursing through her. "Is that why you were chilly toward her? I swear I've only got eyes for you."

She kissed Theo, hands exploring her body and heating her to the core. Theo let out a groan and ran her hands up the backs of Libby's thighs, over the curves of her ass in those tiny, teasing shorts. Their relationship had been developing over the last month and Libby knew just how to touch her to turn her on.

Then Libby stepped away and grinned.

"You are the Joker to my Harley Quinn, after all. There could be no one else," she assured her. "Now come on – let's get back out there and mingle."

They each grabbed a couple of beer bottles and went back to the group to distribute them. Andie was telling Cora and Robin how much Theo had come out of her shell since she'd met Libby.

"I was getting worried that she'd never leave the apartment again," she said. "Her last breakup really did a number on her and I thought she was going full hermit. Her ex-"

Theo hip-checked her hard and Andie stopped talking. She took the beer Theo offered as Theo finished her sentence. "Is ancient history. Anyway, Robin, what kind of conference are you going to?"

"It's a typography summit."

"Robin is a graphic designer," Libby said. "She's really talented – have you seen the cover art for the new Stephen King novel?"

"That was you?" Andie asked, her eyes going wide.

Theo could see exactly where *that* interaction was going. Knowing how passionate Andie could be when she met someone who intrigued her, they'd end up leaving together tonight.

The group broke into separate conversations after a few minutes. Theo put in her time with Robin as promised and she really did warm up after a while – or maybe that was Andie's thinly veiled desire loosening her up. In any case, Theo excused herself to let the new lovebirds get acquainted and wandered the store alone for a few minutes.

Libby was circulating, greeting shivering newcomers as they came into the shop and pointing them to the Halloween-themed tables she'd set up. A few people asked about last-minute costumes and accessories, a lot of them commenting on Libby's perfectly on-point Harley Quinn outfit.

Wherever Theo went in the store, Libby's voice carried, laughing and charming her guests. She really was in her element here, the life of the party. She never forgot about Theo, though, catching her gaze now and again. Every time she did, Theo's desire burned a little hotter.

By midnight, the foot traffic outside the shop dwindled as everyone got to where they were going and the rush of customers who'd come for Libby's party died down. Theo was three beers deep and feeling a warm, tingly buzz that intensified every time Libby walked past and brushed her hand over her vest, or her arm, or her ass.

She enjoyed teasing her. It was working.

Libby let Josie go home, then said to the little group that remained, "Okay, everybody, I think Good Vibes is going to call it a night. Thanks so much for coming out."

"I'll stay and help you clean up," Theo said.

"I can help, too," Robin offered.

"No," Theo and Andie said in unison. Cora and Penny smirked – they'd become fast friends and there was no putting anything past either of them.

"Come on, I'll makes sure you get to your hotel safely," Andie said, pulling Robin toward the door by her rainbow unicorn tail. "Let's all get out of Libby's hair. Thanks so much for the party and the booze!"

"My pleasure," Libby said. "Robin, call me after your conference if you want to get dinner before you go home."

She ushered everyone out of the shop and Theo stood close behind her, the alcohol mixing with the state of constant arousal that Libby had kept her in all night. That and the open, positive environment of Good Vibes gave Theo the courage to drop all pretext. The moment Libby drew the shades and locked the door, Theo pinned her against it.

Libby was already breathing heavy, her chest rising and falling hypnotically. Her lips sought Theo's but first, Theo had to ask the question that had been on her mind all night.

Her whole body was pulsing with desire. She could hardly contain herself. But she held back long enough to ask, "Will you be my girlfriend, Libby?"

Theo looked into her glimmering brown eyes and the whole world paused as she waited for an answer. Libby smirked. "It's about damn time."

She grabbed Theo's hand and put it between her thighs. Theo's desire bubbled over and she hooked the slick fabric of Libby's shorts aside, plunging her fingers into her folds.

"You're so wet."

"Have been ever since you walked in that door."

"God, me too."

Libby undid the buttons of Theo's pants and slid her fingers beneath the waistband of Theo's boxers. Theo buried her face in the curve of Libby's neck as she glided her fingers back and forth through her wetness. She closed her eyes, inhaling the grapefruit scent of her hair as it mingled with the intoxicating smell of her sex.

"I want you," Libby whispered, her voice tickling Theo's ear.

That was it – the final straw.

Theo could not wait a single second longer to take what she wanted.

What she needed.

She spun Libby around and set her on top of the nearest table, knocking all sorts of toys and lubes to the floor in the process. She yanked Libby's pants down to her ankles in one fluid motion and knelt in front of her, burying her face between Libby's thighs.

12

LIBBY

"Oh, Theo," Libby moaned, her fingers tangled up in Theo's hair as her head moved between Libby's thighs. Her arms encircled Libby's hips, pinning her in place as her tongue lapped hungrily at her. "Fuck me."

Theo's blue-gray eyes flitted up to her face, desire sparkling in them, and she ran her hand up and down the slickness between Libby's thighs. When she felt Theo's fingers pressing into her, she shook her head.

"Not like that."

"Hmm?"

Libby sat up, reaching for one of the products still sitting on the table beside her – a box that she tore open in one swift motion. She tossed its contents – a black leather harness – at Theo and gave her a challenging look. "You want to get a little adventurous with me?"

Theo caught the harness and smiled. "I guess I've got

just enough liquid courage in me to try it." She glanced at the Vibe Wall. "Do I pick, or... ?"

Libby nodded. "Take your pick – I've tried them all. I'll consider it a write-off."

Theo let out a nervous laugh. "I'll buy it from you – can't very well contribute to the downfall of your business after all the work we've done building it up."

"I don't think one dildo is going to ruin me."

"Don't be so sure," Theo said, surprising Libby with a sudden burst of confidence. She got to her feet, leaning across the table and pressing her body against Libby's to kiss her.

Then she walked slowly along the Vibe Wall, making her selection while Libby watched and waited. She was slow and methodical about it, stopping here and there to read the reviews Libby and her customers had posted.

The wait was almost unbearable. Libby bit her lip, trying not to squirm under the power of her desire.

Finally, Theo picked a short but thick purple dildo off the wall – one with a powerful vibrator that Libby knew well. She held it up and Libby nodded eagerly. "That's a good one."

"I know," Theo said, tapping a card on the wall. "You gave it five out of five Screaming Orgasms."

She grabbed an unopened box from the shelf beneath the Vibe Wall and tore the dildo out of its packaging as she made her way back over. Libby slid off the table and undressed Theo, peeling her clothes slowly away as she kissed each new area of exposed skin.

Libby helped her into the harness and Theo turned

around to slide the cock into the O-ring. When she turned back, her stare was piercing and it made Libby's whole body thrum with desire. She'd been wanting this from Theo – she knew there was a more adventurous side to her and the fact that she stood tall and wore the strap-on for the first time without giggling or looking mortified confirmed it.

Theo wanted to fuck her just as badly as Libby wanted to be fucked. She'd just needed a little push.

"You are so fucking hot," Libby said, gliding her hands down Theo's small breasts.

She ran them around Theo's hips next and squeezed her ass. Theo backed her up until her thighs were pressing against the table and the strap-on pressed into the crease of her legs. Libby let out a whimper, wanting more, and Theo bent to lift her by her thighs.

She set Libby back on the table and buried her face in the crook of her neck while she moved the silicon cock up and down Libby's folds, wetting it with her juices.

"Tell me you want me," she murmured against Libby's skin.

"I do," she said. Each stroke intensified the heat in Libby's core and she could barely think for wanting her. "Theo, you're amazing and you make me so hot."

Her hands went to Libby's breasts, squeezing, kneading and pinching at her nipples. Every touch sent lightning bolts of arousal through her body and Libby clung to Theo. Her thighs wrapped around her hips and their bodies met.

She felt so good, warmth and softness contrasting with the hardness that pressed between Libby's thighs.

"Fuck me, baby," she repeated. "I need you."

Theo teased her. She closed her fist around the base of the dildo, the sight sending a shiver through Libby. Then she glided it slowly up and down the length of Libby's folds. She made sure it was completely slick with her juices and Libby's body was throbbing for it by the time Theo slid into her.

Libby cried out, her fingernails digging into Theo's shoulders as she clung to her. Theo moved in and out of her, small strokes that turned into long ones, and their hips moved in perfect rhythm.

Theo hooked one arm under Libby's leg, widening her hips so she could penetrate her a little deeper. Their hips connected and bliss bloomed through Libby's body like a ripple on the surface of calm water.

But there was nothing calm about this.

"Hang on a second," Libby said. She reached between her legs, finding a small button at the base of the dildo. She looked into Theo's eyes as she pressed it, the sudden vibration making them both moan. "Is that okay?"

"Fantastic."

Theo started fucking her harder, faster, the sensation of the vibrating base of the dildo against her clit multiplying and intensifying as her face screwed up in a symphony of ecstasy.

Libby reached down to roll a finger over her own clit. She couldn't remember the last time she was this wet, this turned on. Certainly not when she'd been riding the purple appendage alone.

"How does it feel?" she asked.

Theo's eyes had partly rolled back in her head. Her mouth was open and she struggled to find words – they were practically redundant by the time she finally managed to say, "Good. Really good."

"Can you come like this?"

"Yes," Theo said, her voice shaky. "I'm close."

"Me, too. Come with me."

She kept rolling her finger over her clit in fast circles as Theo pumped in and out of her, groaning louder and louder with each thrust of her hips against the vibrating base of the dildo.

"Harder," Libby said. Her whole body was shaking and Theo bucked her hips frantically against her, chasing her own orgasm.

"Oh, fuck," she groaned, her body tightening against Libby's grasp. They clung to each other, their hips moving and grinding against the vibrations, as they came together in one shuddering, mind-blowing orgasm.

Then Theo pulled out and Libby reached down, turning off the vibration and yanking the straps of the harness loose. The whole thing fell to the floor in a heap and Libby slid off the table, wrapping her arms around Theo.

Her body felt so perfect against Libby's nakedness, her chest rising and falling rapidly as she worked to regain her breath.

"Was it good for you?" Theo asked, a little self-consciousness creeping back into her voice.

"Amazing," Libby said. "It'll be even better if I can persuade you to come upstairs for a little post-coital snuggling, though. What do you think?"

"Sure," Theo said. She gathered up their clothes and Libby grabbed the harness, giving her a wink.

"Just in case we want it for round two."

They went upstairs and Libby led Theo into the bedroom. They lay down in the bed and Theo wrapped Libby up in her arms, showering her shoulders, neck and ears in kisses as Libby relaxed against her.

"Mm, that feels nice."

"You feel nice," Theo said, her hand straying to Libby's full chest. As she cupped one breast in her hand, making warmth bloom between Libby's thighs all over again, she said, "I'm really proud of you, by the way."

Libby snorted because she'd just been thinking the same thing about Theo stepping outside of her comfort zone with the strap-on. "What for?"

"You're doing a really great job with Good Vibes," Theo said. "The party tonight was a huge success. There must have been at least a hundred people who dropped in."

"Josie said we did good business tonight," Libby said. "Maybe holiday events can be my differentiating factor to compete with all the online retailers."

She looked over her shoulder, waiting to see if Theo would be as impressed with the growth of her business vocabulary as she was. Theo hugged her tighter and said, "Your differentiator is empowerment."

"Huh?"

"At SexyCon, you said you approach every customer by asking how you can empower them to feel good about their bodies and their love lives," she said. "That's a fantastic mission statement."

Libby laughed and twisted around in Theo's arms to face her. "Does your mind ever stop working?"

"Nope – overthinking is *my* differentiator."

Libby snuggled against her chest, enjoying the soft curves of Theo's breasts against her cheek. She closed her eyes, inhaling her scent, and surrendered to the moment.

Then Theo asked, "So tell me more about Robin." Libby raised her head to look at her, so Theo added, "It seems like Andie fell pretty hard in lust for her tonight, and unless I was reading things wrong, you had a crush on her, too, once upon a time. Is she always that bewitching?"

Libby laughed. "Robin, bewitching? No, that's not a word I'd use to describe her."

"But you don't deny the crush."

"Doesn't everyone fall in love with their best friend at some point?" Libby asked. "Haven't you ever thought about dating Andie?"

Theo laughed. "The girl who wet my bed during a sleepover when we were seven and who has to be reminded to close the bathroom door when she's on the toilet? No, I know way too much about her to be in love with her."

"Does that mean you'll end things with me if I pee with the door open?"

"Of course not," Theo said. "But let's try to keep the mystery alive at least a little longer, okay?"

"Deal." Libby snuggled back against Theo, kissing the dimple at the base of her neck. "I *did* have a crush on Robin when we were kids, but that was because I thought we were the same – kindred spirits."

"And you weren't?"

"No," Libby said. "I didn't discover until freshman year of college that she secretly wanted to be normal."

Theo let out an exaggerated gasp. "That monster."

Libby batted at her head. "It *was* monstrous. I applied to all the same schools as she did. I thought we were going to go to college together and once we weren't long-distance anymore, we would finally be able to date. Then Robin picked the only school I didn't get into and when I asked her why she did that, she said it had the best graphic design program. I wouldn't have held it against her if that was true, but every school she applied to had great programs."

"So what happened?"

"We drifted apart," Libby said. "She didn't have time for me anymore and we went from talking every day for hours to emailing each other a couple times a week. I decided to surprise her with a visit while I was on Thanksgiving break and I found her strolling across campus holding hands with some girl and wearing *Greek letters.*"

She said the last part with dramatic flair and Theo

widened her eyes. "Not Greek letters. Anything but Greek letters."

"What's more normal than pledging a sorority?" Libby said. "Meanwhile, there *I* was, standing in front of her wearing rainbow-colored eye shadow and reminding her of the freak she'd been all through childhood. She distanced herself from me because she wanted to be a different person in college, and the sad thing is that I know she still loves to dress up. You saw how happy she was in that unicorn costume. But that was just because it's Halloween. The rest of the year, she dresses like the same boring, suit-wearing corporate drones as everyone else because she bought into the lie that it's how you *have* to dress. Now we see each other once or twice a year and we're still good friends, but it's not the same anymore."

"That *is* sad," Theo agreed. "What do you think made Robin stop while you managed to stay true to yourself?"

Libby glanced over Theo's shoulder to the mirrored closet door on the wall. Her Harley Quinn dye job was just visible in the low light and the first thing that came to mind was, *Because I'm afraid of being boring.*

"I guess she just outgrew that phase," Libby said instead. "Maybe I still need it."

Theo always seemed to know when to push and when to let her off the hook. She took the cue effortlessly now, pulling Libby into a fierce hug and saying, "I think you're perfect just as you are. Hey, I had an idea. What do you and your mom do for Thanksgiving?"

"Not much," Libby said. "We usually make reservations at a restaurant in the city."

"What about coming to my family's cabin upstate?" Theo asked. "My mom and aunts always go all-out with the food. Penny and Andie will be there, and you can meet Penny's fiancé, Chet. He's like a character study in suit-wearing corporate drones. And my parents have been asking to meet you. I'm sure they'd love to have two extra guests."

Libby smiled. "You told your parents about me?"

"You made me go to a sex convention the first time I met your mom and you're surprised I mentioned you to mine?"

"Oh, you had fun," Libby teased. "Okay, let's do Thanksgiving with your family."

"Great," Theo said, her eyes following Libby as she crawled toward the foot of the bed. "Where are you going?"

Libby snagged the harness off the floor, dangling it from her index finger. "Round two?"

Theo sat up and grabbed Libby by the waist, pulling her back into bed with a yelp of joy.

13

THEO

Theo and Libby rode up to the Catskills in the back seat of Penny's little subcompact, laughably squeezed in with Andie like sardines.

Chet was driving and Penny was talking a mile a minute about cake tasting and the catering options they'd checked out the previous week. Theo managed to maneuver one hand onto Libby's knee.

"Are you *sure* your mom doesn't want to join us?" she asked as they turned onto Route 87, which would take them all the way into the mountains. "It's not too late to pick her up."

"Where would she sit?" Andie asked with a snort. "In the trunk?"

"She's fine," Libby said. "We've never been big holiday celebrators and I think she's just happy to have a day to sleep in and relax."

"Well, we'll have to make sure we spend Christmas with her," Theo said.

She nestled against Libby – as much as one could nestle with one's shoulders pinned on both sides – and tried to enjoy the ride. It was about two and a half hours to her parents' cabin in the mountains where they liked to host Thanksgiving each year, and for once, Theo's heart wasn't racing. Her stomach wasn't churning at the idea of such a long trip. Her mind wasn't screaming for her to find an exit strategy *and fast*.

She was just present. Libby's warmth pressed up against her, Andie was dancing in her seat to some Nat Butler song playing through her headphones, and Penny was chattering away about salmon and steak entrees.

Libby had been teaching Theo how to do that – to just *be* – and it sure was nice when she could manage it.

That sense of calm disappeared the moment the five of them set foot in the log cabin in the woods. Theo's mother came out of the kitchen covered in flour, her dad and two uncles were screaming at a game playing on the radio, and there were four little terrors – Theo's cousins – running circles around the cabin in a spirited game of tag.

"Tag me in!" Andie said, jumping right into the fray. One of Theo's cousins obliged and she ran after him through the dining room.

"That one never changes," Theo's mom said, laughing. "Theodora, Penelope, my babies. You need to visit more!" She pulled them each into a hug, then smiled and said, "And this must be Libby."

She wiped her hands on her apron and when she tried to shake, Libby pulled her into a hug instead. "It's so nice to meet you, Mrs. Kostas."

"Oh, call me Cassandra," she said. "Well, that's a beautiful skirt."

She held Libby at arm's length to take her in. She wore a thick-cabled skirt she'd knitted out of yarn in brilliant oranges and deep reds to match the season, with little applique leaves along the hem. "Thank you, I made it myself."

"Libby's really crafty," Theo said. "She makes a lot of her own clothes."

"I don't suppose that skill extends to pie crusts?" her mom asked. "I always struggle with lattice tops."

"I could give it a shot," Libby offered, and before she'd even finished talking, Theo's mom was whisking her into the kitchen to join Theo's aunts.

"Are you coming, dear?" she called over her shoulder. "Penelope, you too."

"Duty calls," Penny said, leaving Chet with the men gathered around the radio.

Theo followed the other women into the kitchen, which looked a little like a bomb full of baking supplies had gone off there. Libby had wasted no time and was already diving into the dough for the pie lattice.

"Well, there's my favorite niece!" Aunt Cynthia said, looking up from a pot of soup on the stove.

"Who?" Penny asked. "Me or Theo?"

"Yes," Cynthia said with a wry smile. "Now come help me season the *avgolemono*."

"Yes, ma'am," Theo said. "Tasting – now that's something I can handle."

The meal was just as chaotic as the prep work but Libby held her own throughout the day. She managed to get a few words in edge-wise even in the midst of Theo's chatty aunts, she'd won the kids over when she taught them how to fold their cloth napkins into colorful sailor hats, and she'd even impressed Theo's dad with her entrepreneurial spirit.

Theo held her breath when he asked – across the dinner table no less – what exactly Libby's business was.

"I run a boutique adult store," she said, then winked at Theo and added the mission statement they'd come up with together. "With a focus on female empowerment."

"Oh," Theo's dad said, unpacking the words for a moment and finally deciding he approved. "That sounds nice, dear. Can someone pass me the mashed potatoes?"

Theo tried not to snicker and Libby leaned in to whisper to her. "Do you think he knows what I meant?"

"Let's pray that he doesn't."

After the meal, everyone was full and happy, and a lot of the anticipatory energy that filled the cabin before had been spent. People found places to relax and digest, and Theo took Libby by the hand.

"Up for a little walk?"

"Sure, if it's actually a little one," Libby said, one hand on her belly. "I really shouldn't have had that *third* helping of your aunt's lemon chicken soup."

"But she loves you like a daughter since you did."

"Is that the way to your family's hearts?" Libby asked. "Through *my* stomach?"

Theo laughed. "You could say that. But I'm pretty sure everybody already loves you so you don't need to worry about that."

The most beautiful blush came to Libby's skin and Theo had to stop and kiss her right there in the living room. Not a single one of her family members noticed – they were all in a post-meal tryptophan haze.

"Come on."

Theo took her outside, where the light was just beginning to go pink and orange in a beautiful mountain sunset. The cabin was nestled on the side of a hill with a spectacular view of the forest beyond, but Theo's favorite thing was the little pond at the back of the property.

She led Libby on a slightly overgrown path around the side of the cabin and down a slight incline. Five minutes later, they were standing on a ten-foot-wide boulder overlooking the pond.

"We came out to the cabin a lot during the summers when I was a kid. I used to come out to this boulder all the time. It's so peaceful," she said as she pulled Libby down to sit. They let their legs dangle and Libby looked over. The drop was only about five feet to the surface of the water.

"How deep is it?" Libby asked. "Ever go diving?"

Theo shook her head. "Never felt like breaking my neck. It's about waist-deep – Penny and I would get pool floats and spend whole afternoons just bobbing along on the water."

"It's beautiful," Libby said. "The whole place is breathtaking."

"As are you," Theo said.

She laced her hands on either side of Libby's neck and pulled her in for a kiss. They lingered there, making the moment last because no one could see them through the brush and because it was quiet for the first time since they'd arrived.

"I really like you," Theo said when she released her. She'd been meaning to say more than that – the other L word had been dancing on the tip of her tongue a lot lately – but at the last minute, she lost her nerve.

"I really like you, too," Libby said, kissing her again.

"What do you think of my family?"

Libby smiled. "They're great. Not a single one of them ever shuts up, but I guess that's why you turned out to be the strong, silent type most of the time."

Theo laughed. "Yeah, now that you mention it, maybe that's a coping mechanism." She frowned. She'd meant it as a joke, but actually, that sounded *exactly* right.

"What?"

"I was just remembering something..."

"Tell me."

"You know my mom's a nurse, right?"

Libby nodded. "She told me all about her twenty years on the pediatric ward while we were latticing the pies."

"I just had this really vivid memory of what it was

like when I got sick as a kid," Theo said. "I can practically taste the ginger ale."

Libby laughed. "I could definitely see Cassandra as the doting type."

"It was more than that," Theo said. "What did your mom do when you were sick?"

Libby shrugged. "Took my temperature, gave me fluids, and told me to see the school nurse if I felt like puking."

"Not mine," Theo said. "She'd turn my whole bedroom into a sick bay – humidifier, Vicks, every type of medication the drug store carried, blankets, chicken noodle soup – the works. Every illness was a catastrophe that required bedrest. And she always went out and bought me a new card game to keep me occupied while I convalesced."

"She sounds really comforting," Libby said, wrapping her arm around Theo's waist and resting her head on her shoulder while they watched the sun setting over the water.

"She was," Theo agreed. "Maybe a little too much."

"Why do you think she was like that? Just because she's a nurse?"

"No," Theo said. "I'm sure it was because of my sister. Did I tell you she almost died when I was seven?"

"No!" Libby sat up, alarm in her eyes. "What happened?"

"We were at summer camp," Theo said. "It was my first year there and I was so excited – Penny's two years older than me and she always told me how amazing it was, so I had a ton of fun to catch up on. The first three weeks of the summer were a total blast, but then Penny started feeling sick. It was really sudden. I remember her running out of the dining hall at breakfast with her hand over her mouth, and by the afternoon my counsellor was calling me out of the swimming area to meet Penny in the medical cabin."

"What was wrong with her?"

"Appendicitis," Theo said. "It came on so quickly, it scared the hell out of me – and the counsellors too, I think. Our parents were going to come pick us both up and take Penny to the hospital but they were over three hours away and she just kept getting sicker and sicker. The camp nurse finally decided Penny couldn't wait any longer and she called to have her life flighted out of the camp, with me along for the ride. It turned out that her appendix had burst. The doctors told my parents later that she could have gone septic and died if the nurse hadn't called the emergency helicopter to get her to a hospital."

"That sounds terrifying," Libby said. "Especially for a seven-year-old."

"It was," Theo agreed. "It took a long time for Penny to recover and it was terrifying for my parents, too. I'm not sure my mom ever got over the helplessness of being several hours away while her kid was so sick. She always tried to make up for it by being extra-cautious with everything from the common cold to bloody noses."

"It doesn't sound like you ever got over it, either,"

Libby suggested gently. "Do you think that's where your agoraphobia comes from?"

"Definitely," Theo said. "I've worked that much out with my therapist, but there's only so much good it does to know the origin."

"They do say that knowing is half the battle."

"Thanks, Dr. Phil."

Libby scoffed and pretended to reach for Theo like she was going to throw her into the pond. Theo caught her in a hug, pinning her arms to her sides and rendering the threat neutralized, then they nestled together again.

"Thanks for coming here with me," she said. "And meeting my crazy family."

"It was my pleasure," Libby said. "Thanks for inviting me."

"Maybe I'll make an appointment with my therapist when we get home," Theo said. "Find out what comes after *knowing*. Because I'm really enjoying what life looks like with you, Libby. I don't want to screw it up by pushing you away, or being too afraid to leave my apartment."

"Even if you were, I'd come visit you every day."

"Don't say that," Theo teased. "It might happen."

"It won't."

"How can you be so sure?"

"You're so different now than you were when I met you," Libby said. "So much more confident, more relaxed."

"I could relapse."

"You could," Libby agreed. "But you can't scare me away with that talk, Theo. I'm here to stay."

"Good." Theo kissed Libby again, then she heard someone calling their names behind them. "I think it's time for the traditional after-dinner game of Monopoly. Wanna play?"

"Okay," Libby said. Then she was up and dashing off the boulder. "Come on – I gotta get the top hat."

Theo laughed. That girl kept her on her toes, never quite sure what came next, and up until a few months ago, that would have filled her with terror. Now, she couldn't wait to find out.

14

LIBBY

"Do you have this butt plug in black?"

"Absolutely," Libby said. "We've also got it in bright pink and neon green if you want to collect the whole set."

"Do you think this harness will fit me?" another customer asked.

They were three deep around Libby on the sales floor and she was spinning from one person to the next, rattling off answers as fast as she could. It was like a scene out of one of her wildest dreams for Good Vibes, but no, this was actually happening.

She and Josie were deep in the thick of Valentine's season and with Theo's help, Libby had devised a killer marketing and advertising plan to take advantage of any sex shop's most profitable annual event.

Free lube with every toy purchase and a complimentary couples' ticket to attend one of Libby's mom's sex-positive workshops – that was all it took to flood Good

Vibes with customers in February. Libby stood in the middle of the chaos wearing a bright pink tutu and Cupid wings, lapping up every moment of it.

"You're not going to believe this," Josie said on the night of the 14th while Libby locked up the shop.

"What?"

Josie was counting the day's earnings and Libby couldn't help but worry a little bit. There were hardly any toys left on the shelves – her Vibe Wall had been damn near decimated – and yet she'd been struggling for so long, she braced for bad news.

"We're in the black," Josie said. "For the *whole* fiscal year."

"What do you mean?"

"In the black," Josie repeated. "That's a business term for-"

Libby laughed. "I know what 'in the black' means – Theo and I don't get much studying done these days, but she did teach me a few things. We gave away so much lube this month. How could we still have positive cash flow?"

Josie shrugged. "A five-dollar bottle of lube and a seventy-dollar vibrator equals sixty-five dollars in profit. Multiply that by..." She did a quick tally on a statistics sheet Theo had suggested they keep on the checkout counter to keep track of how the sale was going. "...173 toy sales so far this month. Libby, we did *really* well."

Libby just stared at her for a second. *We did really well.* That statement took a minute to compute. Then she let out a whoop and punched at the air.

"That's amazing!" She came around the counter and squeezed Josie in a bear hug so fierce she lifted her feet off the ground. "Thank you so much for your help. You're getting a Valentine's Day bonus, my friend!"

Libby sent Josie home to enjoy what remained of the holiday and she floated through the rest of the closing tasks. The grin never left her lips as she went home and changed – transforming from the cutesy Cupid she'd been at work to something more akin to a Victoria's Secret angel for Theo. Then she layered a flowing black dress over her lingerie, put a heavy winter coat on top of that and took the subway to Theo's place.

They'd both agreed it would be best not to make a big deal of their first Valentine's Day together. Libby needed to keep Good Vibes open during the day for last-minute shoppers, and any plans they made that involved reservations or traveling would stress Theo out. When Andie said she'd be out of town on Valentine's Day, that had sounded like the perfect excuse for a romantic night in.

"Are you sure you don't mind keeping it low-key?" Theo had asked when Libby suggested it.

"I really don't," Libby had answered, pinching Theo's cheeks as she kissed her. "All I need is you – not a bunch of candy hearts and prefabricated greeting card sentiments."

The truth was that she loved candy hearts. She loved everything about Valentine's Day but she'd never had anyone to share it with. That was the important part, the person who gave all that store-bought romance real meaning. It scared her a little that Theo was quickly becoming that person for her.

Okay, it scares me more than a little, she admitted to herself as she reached the third-floor landing of Theo's apartment building. There was a rose petal on the floor. Dropped from someone's bouquet? Libby smiled and picked it up.

She rounded the corner into the hallway and found another, then another, placed carefully every foot or so. Libby followed them, expecting the petals to end at someone else's door – a romantic gesture to which she was an unwitting observer.

Instead, they kept going, terminating at apartment 302.

Libby grinned as she put her hand on the unlocked door handle. She went inside, opening her mouth to ask about the rose petals, but what was waiting in the living room stole her breath away.

The lights were turned off and the whole room was illuminated with the warm, flickering glow of dozens of tea candles. There were tapers on the dining table, along with two place settings and a bottle of red wine, and candy hearts sprinkled across the table served as decoration.

Beside the table, Theo stood in a crisp white button-down and a silky tie that gave Libby a strong urge to use it as a leash. She could just picture herself grabbing the tie in her fist and reeling Theo in to her.

"Happy Valentine's Day," Theo said.

"You did all this for me?"

"Let's not lie to ourselves – you are *not* a low-key kind of girl and I wouldn't have you any other way."

"Babe," Libby said, her heart full, racing for Theo. "I can't believe you did this."

"Do you like it?" Theo asked, a frown touching her lips for the first time. She crossed the room to take Libby's hand.

"I love it." She grabbed Theo's tie after all, yanking her down so their lips met. The words were evading her so she tried to let her body tell Theo exactly how happy she was.

Theo groaned – mission accomplished – and murmured against her lips, "Dinner's ready. Should we eat?"

"Yes, please," Libby said, running her hands over Theo's chest. Theo turned toward the kitchen and Libby swatted her ass just for fun, then followed her. "What's on the menu?"

"I can't take credit for it," Theo said. "I ordered delivery from a steakhouse nearby. We've got filets, roasted green beans, mashed potatoes-"

Libby wrapped her arms around Theo from behind and moaned in her ear. "Oh, that sounds so good. I'm starving."

"-and mascarpone-filled, chocolate covered strawberries for dessert."

"I think I just came," she teased.

Theo twisted in her arms. "Won't be the last time tonight if I have anything to say about it." She kissed Libby, then handed her a plate. They went back to the dining table and Theo poured from the wine bottle. "So, don't keep me in suspense. How did the last day of the sale go?"

"*Amazing*," Libby said around a bite of mashed potatoes. She wasn't even sure if she was answering Theo's question or just talking about the food – the superlative applied to both.

She told Theo all about her latest batch of happy customers, as well as Josie's estimation that the sale had put the shop in great financial shape.

"And it's all thanks to you," Libby concluded. "I really couldn't have done any of it without you. If Andie hadn't forgotten her phone accidentally-on-purpose and sent you to fetch it, I'd probably still be scratching my head at balance sheets to this day."

"It was my business knowledge, maybe, but it's your hard work," Theo corrected.

"To Good Vibes," Libby said, raising her wine glass. "And to you."

"To us."

"Even better."

They clinked their glasses together, sending the flames from the taper candles dancing as they drank. After a while, Libby asked Theo about the progress on her game. They'd been working on it together here and there and Theo had the basic structure nailed down. The concept was what would happen if Libby's sex dice slept with *Cards Against Humanity* and their love child was born on the island of Lesbos.

So far, though, the idea hadn't made it any further than a stack of index cards on Theo's desk.

"I haven't had much time what with all the slaving I've done in the kitchen," Theo said with a smirk. "But I wouldn't mind a little help trying out a couple new positions I added to the deck."

"I am your faithful product tester," Libby said. "Use me as you wish."

Theo kicked off her shoe and her bare foot found Libby's beneath the table, her toes gliding up the inside of Libby's leg. They'd made quick work of their dinners and their plates were empty – the wine bottle was, too – and although their dessert awaited them, nothing could have been further from Libby's mind.

She got up, letting her hips sway as she closed the distance between them. She pulled her dress over her head and tossed it into Theo's lap, then enjoyed the warm, tingly sensation of Theo's eyes tracing every curve of her body.

Libby was wearing a black bodice with sheer lace, her breasts nearly spilling over the tight bra cups. Her panties were a matching lace with little satin bows on both her hips and she wore a garter on one thigh which she'd picked up on a whim on her way out of Good Vibes.

Theo hooked her finger in it and let the elastic snap back against Libby's thigh. "Wow. You look incredible."

"Is that all?"

"No," Theo said, her voice already sounding husky with desire. "I've never seen anyone as beautiful and sexy as you. Whenever you're in a room with me, I can't keep my eyes off you. Hell, I can *barely* keep my hands off you." She didn't even try now – she ran her fingers up Libby's thighs and cupped her ass, pulling her closer. "You're smart, you're funny, you're sexy-"

"You said sexy twice."

"I meant it twice," Theo said. She bent and kissed the ridge of Libby's hip bone, then licked the exposed skin at her waist, sending a shiver through her. "If anything, I ought to say it three times. Libby, you are so fucking sexy. I love you."

She closed her teeth around the top of Libby's panties but Libby pushed her away. "What?"

"Huh?"

"You love me?"

Theo's mouth dropped open. "I- yeah. Of course I love you."

She was looking at Libby like it was the most natural thing in the world and not the three most difficult words in the English language.

"I've been wanting to say it for a while," Theo admitted. "I thought we were on the same page but if you're not ready to say it back, that's okay-"

"That's not it."

"So you *do* love me back?"

"I-" Libby was all tongue-tied. "I don't *not* love you. It's just... how can you know?"

"How can I know I love you?"

"Yes."

"I know because ever since I met you, I haven't wanted to let a day go by without talking to you," Theo said, taking Libby's hand and pulling her closer again. She pulled her onto her lap and wrapped her arms around Libby's waist. "I know because my heart tries to climb into my throat every time I see you, and because I can't imagine my life without you. I know because even though it's the most difficult thing I've ever done, you make me want to conquer my anxiety so I can be with you."

"But how do you know you love *me*?"

"I don't follow."

Libby's pulse was racing by now and this was decidedly *not* where she'd seen this evening ending up. They should be in the bedroom by now, tearing each other's clothes off like wild animals. Instead, they'd taken an abrupt detour into the depths of her insecurities.

That was a place she never enjoyed going.

"How can you ever know that the person you love is *really* who you love, and not just a construct they've designed?" she asked. If she were still wearing her Cupid tutu and wings, it might be easier to explain. Perhaps the very fact that she'd been in Cupid wings earlier and it had been so easy to transition into sexy mode would help Theo understand.

"*Are* you a construct?"

"Yes," Libby said. "And no. Not all the time. But the clothes, the hair-" She flipped a lock of bright red hair over her shoulder – it had been red all month in honor of Valentine's Day, but she was already thinking about teal.

"That's all superficial stuff," Theo said. "I didn't fall in love with the color of your hair."

Libby sighed. Theo wasn't getting it, but Libby didn't blame her. Hadn't she been trying as hard as she could to keep up the façade? And now she suddenly expected Theo to look through it and see the scared, uninteresting little girl underneath.

"What if all I am is the color of my hair?" she asked. There it was – her worst fear, uttered by candlelight to a gorgeous woman who'd just fed her a beautiful meal and told Libby she loved her.

"That's impossible," Theo said. "You're so much more than that."

Libby got off Theo's lap and picked up her dress. This wasn't a conversation she could have in her underwear.

"You're not leaving, are you?" Theo asked, looking scared.

Libby glanced toward the door. She'd only meant to get dressed, but now that Theo mentioned it, the idea was tempting. She could just run away, call this yet another casual experiment – albeit a rather long and involved one – and all of it would amount to nothing.

No harm done.

"Don't leave."

The pain in Theo's voice was the only thing that convinced Libby to stay. Maybe she couldn't say it out loud for fear of rejection, but Libby loved Theo, too, and Theo didn't deserve to be walked out on.

"Okay."

"Let's talk, okay?"

Libby nodded and she helped Theo blow out all the

candles, then they went down the hall to her bedroom. They climbed into Theo's bed – there was nowhere else in the room where they could sit together – and Libby allowed Theo to swaddle her in blankets and pull her to her chest.

When Libby didn't speak – couldn't find the words – Theo gently said, "Tell me what's on your mind."

"What if I don't have a personality, underneath it all?" Libby said. "I hide behind wild looks and eccentric clothes, but what if you strip it all away and there's nothing left?"

Theo laughed.

Libby shot her a glare.

"I'm sorry," Theo said. "I didn't mean to make light of the question, but are you serious?"

Another glare. Theo sobered up.

"Why do you think you don't have a personality?" she asked. "Is that even possible?"

"Maybe not, but I could turn out to be mind-numbingly boring once you get to know me."

"Of course you're not," Theo said. "I *do* know you and I've never been so fascinated by anyone in my life. You own a sex shop in East Village, for fuck's sake – what's boring about that?"

Libby didn't answer right away. Theo was jumping at the opportunity to poke holes in her logic, but she wasn't really listening. "I got bullied as a kid. Did you know that?"

"Yeah," Theo said. "Robin mentioned it when I

talked to her at your Halloween party. She said that was the reason you two found each other online."

"That's true," Libby said. "I was the definition of painfully shy. Pretty much just attempted to melt into the walls whenever the other kids said mean things to me. This one kid – Jason, a real asshole – was taunting me after school one day after my dad left my mom. I didn't think anyone at school knew he was gone, but I guess Jason lived in the neighborhood my dad moved into with his new family. New wife, two new kids from her previous marriage, big new house."

"That's awful."

"I was waiting for my mom to pick me up from school and she was running late because she was juggling a new job and night school," Libby went on. "And Jason said, 'Libby's so boring her dad went out and found himself a new daughter'."

"When's your next class reunion?" Theo asked, hugging her tighter. "I'm going to find that asshole and kick him in the balls." Libby couldn't help laughing but Theo said, "I'm serious. What a piece of shit, and the fact that you've been carrying that around with you all these years makes me feel sick. It's not true – not even close."

Libby snuggled against Theo and said, almost inaudibly, "Thank you."

"What your dad did isn't right, either," Theo went on. "But that's his damage, not yours."

"Do you still love me?"

"More than ever. Nothing you say or reveal or do can make me stop loving you, Libby."

"Good," Libby squeaked. Tears threatened and she clung to Theo. "Because I love you too."

"Will you be my date to Penny's wedding?"

Libby smiled and pulled away to look Theo in the eyes. "I kind of assumed I was already invited."

Theo kissed her. "Of course. But I never formally asked. It freaks me out to plan things in advance, but I'm saying it now – I want you there."

"Then of course I will be your date," Libby said. "Thank you."

15

THEO

Theo's stomach was twisting and she felt lightheaded.

None of that was new – she'd been feeling that way since the moment she set foot inside JFK International Airport and she'd been working hard to suppress the anxiety for weeks before that.

Penny's bachelorette excursion to Las Vegas had been gnawing at her stomach since the moment Theo found out about it and now all that anxiety was finally due in full.

"How ya doing?" Libby asked, her arm looped in Theo's as they disembarked the plane in Las Vegas.

"I'm okay," Theo lied. She was having a hard time drawing a full breath.

It had been Penny's idea to invite her. She was completely unwilling to bend on the subject of Theo's attendance, but when it came to Libby, Penny had said it was the more, the merrier. It helped that Libby had taken on a mythic status in the Kostas family – she'd gotten Theo to come out of her shell so much in the past few months and Penny probably knew that bringing her to Vegas was the best chance to get Theo through the weekend without a mental breakdown.

Libby was perfect in her role as Theo's emotional support human. She stuck right by her side through both airports and petted Theo's arm during takeoff and landing. And she was so damn excited about the trip that she made Theo want to suck it up and just be normal for once.

"I've never been to Vegas," Libby said, the biggest grin on her face as the four of them – Penny, Andie, Theo and Libby – found their way through McCarran Airport's crowded concourse to the taxi line outside. "Bucket list goal achieved – thanks so much for bringing me along, Penny."

"Are you excited?" Andie asked the bride-to-be, rubbing her hands together. "What kind of debauchery should we get into first?"

"I'm *so* excited," Penny said. "Although we should probably check into the hotel before we get into any debauchery."

"Good call," Andie said. "We have to get you decked out in your bachelorette sash, tiara and Mardi Gras beads in the shape of dicks that we picked up from Libby's shop. You straight girls are odd ones when it comes to getting married – what is it with those phallic objects?"

"Please tell me you didn't actually buy that stuff," Penny groaned.

"We raided my bachelorette inventory," Libby said. "There won't be a person on the Strip who doesn't know you're getting hitched."

They got in a taxi. Theo's hips were smashed against the door and the other girls chattered excitedly the whole way to the hotel. Theo barely heard them over the cacophony in her own head, as well as the visual overload of lights and people on the Strip.

Practice being present in the moment. That was the advice her therapist had given Theo when she'd met with her last week. Theo had gone into her office hoping for a miracle advancement in anti-anxiety medication, some new pill that would let her be as carefree and fun as Libby without the need to sleep for twenty-four hours after the danger passed.

Or maybe her therapist would have a magic bullet, a little nugget of wisdom that would make Theo's anxiety vanish into thin air and lift the burden she'd been carrying for so long. It had been a while since her last appointment so anything was possible.

Being present was all she got, though – that and a follow-up appointment to debrief after the trip was over. A lot of good that advice did... Libby already lived her life completely in the moment and if Theo knew how to copy that attitude, she would have done it already.

"Babe?"

"Huh?"

"You were spacing out," Libby said, rubbing Theo's arm. "Doing okay?"

"Sure." If *okay* meant feeling pretty certain she was about to lose control of her body. "I'm sorry. I wish I could just stop worrying and be excited like everybody else."

"Why don't you?" Libby asked, and Theo couldn't help a flash of annoyance wash over her face.

"Yeah, because it's that simple."

Libby looked a little hurt and if Theo could have taken it back, she would have sucked those cynical words right back into her mouth. But she couldn't and Libby smiled, but the pain stayed in her eyes as she changed the subject.

"I can't believe we're staying in the Bellagio."

"Only the best for my bestie," Andie said. "Now, I brought spending money for the bride-to-be." She wrestled her wallet out of the carry-on backpack at her feet and handed a fat wad to Penny in the front passenger seat. "A hundred bucks in singles should get you through tonight at least. Whether you want to use that on the slots or the exotic dancers, we won't judge."

Penny laughed. "Maybe a combination of both."

"Really?" Andie asked. "Cut loose, Pen. You know what they say about what happens in Vegas."

They got checked into the hotel and went up to the suite Andie had picked out. It was large, with two California king-sized beds, a separate living area and a kitchenette – more than they needed for one weekend, but luxurious and beautiful.

Theo had put up most of the money for the suite. One thing a hermit with no social life had was an excess of funds and even though actually *going* to Vegas was like something out of an Escher nightmare to her, bankrolling it was easy.

"Oh wow," Penny said, throwing her arms wide and flopping backward on the bed. "I'm going to sleep like a baby tonight."

"Later!" Andie said, opening her backpack and dumping the contents onto the other bed. "Get up – we gotta dress you, then we're going to..." She paused for dramatic effect. "...the Top of the World."

"The rotating restaurant?" Libby asked.

"No way!" Penny said. "Awesome."

She was up and digging through the accessories Andie brought, obviously more excited about wearing the *Bride to Be* sash than she let on earlier. Theo was, once again, the only one who wasn't excited. "We didn't discuss that, Andie."

Andie, Penny and Theo had sat down and planned out the entire itinerary for the weekend while they were making their reservations and travel plans. Penny had conceded the element of surprise in exchange for getting Theo on the plane to Las Vegas because the more she knew about what was going to happen and when, the more in control she felt. But now Andie was changing the plans and Theo's anxiety ratcheted up another notch.

Andie gave Theo a dismissive shrug. "Yeah, I thought it'd be a fun surprise. We couldn't very well tell the future Mrs. Winston *everything* to expect on her getaway weekend, could we?"

That meant there could be more surprises hidden under Andie's cap. Great – they'd dragged her here under false pretenses and now they were going off-script. Theo's stomach twisted again, giving a lurch this time for good measure.

She ran into the bathroom, locking the door behind her. Libby followed and called through the door but Theo didn't answer. She went to the sink and splashed water on her face and neck. The suite was perfectly temperature-controlled and yet it felt like her skin was about a hundred and ten degrees. Her heart was pounding again.

Dinner was going to be in an airborne, spinning restaurant with the city becoming a dizzying blur of neon lights below. After that, they'd go into the fray, with crowds and noises and overwhelming sights. Gambling, drinking, straying further and further from the temporary safe space of the hotel suite...

Theo braced her hands against the edge of the sink, her head spinning. What made her think she could handle this?

"Theo?" It was Penny this time, not Libby. Just as well – Penny was already used to a lifetime of cancelled plans and disappointments so she wouldn't fight Theo as much as Libby probably would.

"I'm not feeling well," she called back. "I think you three should go to the restaurant without me. I'll catch up with you after."

Or not, but she'd cross that bridge when it came.

"Do you need anything?" Penny asked. "Is it your stomach?"

"I'll be okay," Theo called. "You have fun – don't worry about me."

There was a pause. She could feel her sister's disappointment radiating through the door. Penny's voice was clipped when she answered. "Okay. We'll text you when we're leaving the restaurant."

Theo heard the suite door open, then close, and then it was quiet. The dizziness subsided, along with the nausea, and all she had left was a pit in her stomach that said, *Great, you fucked up yet again.*

They'd been in Vegas less than an hour before her anxiety smacked her down... maybe her therapist would agree that even getting to Vegas had been a little bit of forward progress.

Maybe not.

"Theo?" Libby's voice was gentle when she called through the door. "Can I come in?"

Theo looked at herself in the mirror, face dripping with water. Pitiful. She blotted her face with a hand towel, then reluctantly opened the door. "I thought you went to dinner with Andie and Penny."

"I couldn't leave you here."

"But now you don't get to eat at the Top of the World."

Libby shrugged. "I wouldn't have enjoyed it knowing you were locked in a bathroom and feeling miserable."

She took Theo's hand and Theo let her lead the way

into the living area. They sank down on a plush leather couch and Theo sighed. "Are you sure you love me? This is what it's going to be like all the time – cancelled plans and panic attacks."

"Why do you limit yourself like that?"

Theo frowned. That wasn't the response she was expecting. "What do you mean?"

"You tell yourself you can't do things, so you make it true," Libby said. "And I think telling me that's all I can ever expect is actually just you trying to push me away. Well, it's not going to work, babe. I refuse to buy into your self-imposed limitations."

"Am I supposed to just turn that part of my brain off?"

"Yes," Libby said. "Yes, you are, because that part of your brain is a liar. What makes your bedroom in New York safe, but the Top of the World unsafe?"

"Well, the Top of the World spins, you have to take an elevator to get to the dining room, that elevator could break down and trap you-"

"And what makes the elevator unsafe?" Libby interrupted Theo's stream of worries. "You could just as easily get sick in your bedroom as in an elevator. Your body doesn't know the difference."

"I get all that," Theo said. "Rationally, it makes sense. But you have no idea how jealous I am that you, Andie and Penny can all just go where you want and do what you want without a constant nagging fear that something horrible is about to happen. Sometimes I really wish I could just stop being me so these thoughts would go away."

Tears threatened, making her vision blurry, and Libby hugged her. "So don't be you."

"What?"

"Just for tonight," Libby said, pulling back to look Theo in the eyes. She wiped the tears from Theo's cheeks. "Give yourself a break from all that exhausting bullshit and be someone else. Here." She pulled her t-shirt over her head and held it out to Theo. "Be me."

Theo smiled uncertainly. "Be you?"

The t-shirt was a size too small, bright pink with the words *I AM what happens in Vegas* printed in gold. Libby stood up and unbuttoned her pants – a snakeskin pattern that was quintessentially Libby and not at all Theo's style. "I'm serious. Get out of your head for the night and just be silly, carefree Libby. I give you permission to take a break from your lying brain."

"This is ridiculous," Theo pointed out.

"Yeah, it probably is," Libby agreed. "Now give me your shirt."

They swapped clothes and Libby dragged Theo back into the bathroom so they could gawk at themselves in the full-length mirror. She laughed and ruffled Theo's neatly combed hair.

"I'd never wear it so neat," she explained. Then she kissed Theo and added, "But it looks great on you normally."

"Thanks," Theo said, laughing. She couldn't resist

throwing a jab back Libby's way. "Well, I would have left butterfly hairclips in the 90s where they belong."

She pulled one of them out of Libby's hair and set it on the counter for when they resumed their own identities later. Libby feigned offense, then she rose onto her toes and kissed Theo again. "I think we're ready. How do you feel?"

"Surprisingly, I think it's helping. I feel okay."

They went downstairs to the casino and played the slot machines until Andie and Penny finished dinner. The four of them met up at the bar an hour later and Andie raised her eyebrows at their wardrobe change.

"Umm, what were you two doing that was more important than dinner?"

"It's not what it looks like," Theo said.

"Just roll with it," Libby said. "It got her out of the hotel room."

"Can't argue with that," Penny said, her mouth a thin line. She was still angry and rightfully so.

"Is it time to get drunk and make it rain?" Andie asked.

"Only if you never say it like that again," Theo teased.

They ordered drinks, exchanged some cash for casino chips, then headed back into the bright lights, ringing bells and constant flow of bodies on the casino floor. Theo didn't mind it as much anymore. Whenever the panic began to rise in her throat, she looked down at her pink t-shirt and remembered that she was Libby, just for tonight.

Libby lived in the moment and in that moment, she was okay.

It took Theo about an hour to find Penny again after she disappeared into the crowd. She finally found her at a roulette table and Theo put a few chips on the table so she could stand beside her.

"Hey."

"Hey."

"How was the restaurant?"

"Really good," Penny said. "You missed out."

"I know," Theo answered, watching the roulette wheel spin. Bust. She put down another chip. "I'm really sorry. Not just for tonight – for every event I've ruined with my anxiety. I try-"

"I know you do. I appreciate you being here with me this weekend," Penny said, putting her arm around Theo's shoulder. "I love you, little sis."

"I love you, too."

"What's it like?"

Penny had never actually asked her about her anxiety before.

Thanks to Libby, Theo actually had the words to explain it. She repeated a lot of what she'd said in the hotel room and she told Penny about the invisible monster that no one else could see.

"When we were kids and you got sick at camp, I was so scared," she said. "I thought you were going to die, but you were fine the day before. I remember that so clearly – you were playing flashlight tag with your friends in the third-grade cabin and you said I was too little to play."

Penny laughed. "Sorry about that."

"It's okay, I was a pest," Theo conceded. "You were fine and then you weren't, and I thought I lost you."

"Well, I'm not going anywhere," Penny said.

Theo took a deep breath, glanced down at her pink shirt, and answered, "Neither am I."

16

LIBBY

Theo seemed calmer after they got back from their Vegas weekend.

Luckily, what happened in Vegas didn't stay there in regards to her mental state, and it seemed like she was able to work through some things with her therapist's guidance afterward, too. One thing Theo was more than ready to leave in Vegas was her temporary Libby persona – she gave back the bright pink t-shirt at the end of the trip.

"I thought it was a ridiculous idea, but pretending to be you really helped," Theo said. "Thank you."

"You just had to get out of your head," Libby said. Then she winked. "Besides, role playing is always fun."

After Penny's bachelorette party, Theo got busy helping her sister with last-minute preparations for the wedding. There were only two and a half months left and it seemed like there was exponentially more to do. Libby was happy to see Theo stepping out of her comfort zone more and more to immerse herself in the wedding plans, but in May, she asked Theo to take a Sunday off from the hustle and bustle.

Libby's mom was approaching retirement at about the same speed that Penny and Chet were approaching the altar and she'd mentioned downsizing a few times. Now the move was imminent and Libby had to take what she wanted before her mom sold off all the excess stuff she'd acquired over the years.

"Come to my mom's house with me," Libby had begged Theo. "We can sort through my childhood bedroom and you can see the environment that shaped the woman who stands before you."

She said it with a flourish, spinning the hand-sewn, fringed skirt she wore. Theo said she'd love to and that was how they'd ended up drinking coffee on the front porch of a little bungalow in Brooklyn around eleven a.m. on a Sunday. It was still early and they were waiting for Libby's mom to come back from the truck rental place.

When she pulled up to the curb in a box truck, Libby and Theo stood up and her mom jumped down from the cab.

"Anything that doesn't make it into the truck is going into the yard sale," she said. "So look through your stuff carefully."

Her mom opened the back of the truck then started carrying boxes out of the house. She'd already packed up most of the rooms, leaving Libby to go through her things that morning.

Theo offered to help Libby's mom carry boxes, but

she said she'd rented the box truck for the whole weekend. "I'm in no great rush. You two have fun with your trip down memory lane."

"I can't believe you're moving out," Libby said. "This has been *home* for so long."

"It's time for a change of scenery," her mom answered. "The neighborhood's been getting more expensive for years and I could get a very nice apartment outside the city for what this house will fetch."

Libby sighed and her mom disappeared into the house for another load of boxes. She asked Theo, "You ready?"

Theo nodded and they went inside. Libby took Theo's hand and led her down the narrow hallway to her bedroom at the back of the house. As she pushed the door open, Theo laughed.

"What?"

"It's just as wild and colorful as I expected."

"It's maybe just a *little* bit of overkill," Libby acknowledged, looking around at the zebra print curtains, the tie-dyed comforter on the bed and the purple walls. Her old desktop computer – where she'd spent countless hours chatting with Robin – still sat on a cheap desk in the corner. "This is where I figured out who I was – the wild and colorful Libby you know and love. Cut me a little slack for the learning curve."

"Fair enough." Theo sat on the bed and Libby smiled.

"What?"

"Nothing," she said, her cheeks coloring. "I just like

the sight of you on my bed. It's like a teenage fantasy come to life."

Theo's eyes flicked toward the open door, then back to Libby. "You ever bring a girl back to your bedroom when you were younger?"

"You're kidding, right?" Libby said. "Nobody wanted me back then."

"Maybe they never told you so," Theo said. "But I refuse to believe no one wanted you. I've never seen you walk into a room without turning a few heads. I think you underestimate the effect you have on people."

"Is that so?" Libby asked, coming closer. Theo took her hand and pulled her close, wrapping her arms around Libby's thighs and resting her chin on her belly as she looked into her eyes.

"Yes. It makes me jealous sometimes."

"Well, I'm all yours," Libby said, bending down to kiss her. Theo slipped her tongue between Libby's lips and warmth bloomed between her thighs. Just as Libby was pressing her body against Theo, about to crawl into bed with her, her mom dropped a box in the other room and cursed.

Libby broke away with a giggle. "Help me go through my things and I'll think up a creative reward for your service."

"Yes, ma'am."

They spent the next hour sorting through Libby's childhood bedroom, reducing it to a pile of cardboard boxes – a few destined for the moving truck but most of them piled against the wall for the yard sale. It was bittersweet – her teenage years certainly hadn't been Libby's favorites, but there were memories of making friends with Robin here, and plenty of good memories with her mom. If she could erase the black hole her father made when he'd left, it would be a pretty darn good childhood.

"Whoa," Theo said as she sorted through Libby's closet. "What is *this*?"

Libby turned to see. "Oh my God. My Victorian dress!"

Theo pulled it out of the closet and Libby took it, laying it across the bed. It looked so small now even though the pattern had been slightly too big on her when she was ten. All the stitching was just as rough and uneven as she remembered, but the dress as a whole looked surprisingly good.

It had a pink crushed velvet bodice with ribbons criss-crossing the chest, and there were long princess sleeves that Libby remembered having a lot of fun with – they'd flowed and moved around her whenever she gestured with her hands. The body of the dress was white lace, with many layers of tulle to give it volume.

"I bet you were adorable as a little kid," Theo said.

"The most adorable," Libby confirmed. She picked the dress up again and held it to her chest to look in the mirror on her door. "You know what? This would make an awesome costume for Pride next month."

Theo raised her eyebrows.

"You don't think so?"

"I don't think you'll fit."

"Challenge accepted," Libby said. She draped the

costume on top of the small pile of things she was planning to take back to her apartment. Everything else she wanted to keep would go into a storage closet at her mom's new apartment. "With a little creative tailoring, there's plenty of tulle there to turn that into a world-class rainbow tutu."

It took about three hours to finish sorting through Libby's things. She was just taking down the zebra print curtains when her mom came and leaned in the doorway. She mopped her brow with the hem of her t-shirt and asked, "How's it going in here, sweetie?"

"Just about done," Libby said. "How about you?"

"Done for now. Do you two want some food? I already packed the kitchen up but I can order a pizza."

"I'd love a pizza," Theo said.

About twenty minutes later, they wound up back on the porch, paper plates in their laps as they enjoyed the fresh air and ate. They were all ravenous from the work and scarfed their first slices in silence, then Libby's mom asked, "How are things going at Good Vibes these days? I miss my workshop ladies – can't wait to get back in there after all this moving business is behind me."

"They're eager to have you back, too," Libby said. "Things are going well. I told you our Valentine's sale put us in the black for the year."

"That's great, sweetie," her mom said. "What about Pride? Did you make a plan to take advantage of that, too?"

"We sure did," Theo said, putting her arm around Libby's waist. "Although it was pretty much all her doing.

She bought advertising space on the light pole banners all the way down the street and we've got screen-printed t-shirts with the Good Vibes logo and website so we can represent the business at Pride."

"That sounds wonderful," Libby's mom said. Was that a touch of astonishment in her eyes?

Libby could hardly blame her mother if she was skeptical about Libby's ability to take the reins on her business. She'd been skeptical herself until Theo stepped in to help.

"What about inventory?" her mom asked. "Are you all stocked up for when your flood of new customers come in?"

"Oh yeah," Theo said. Sometimes Libby wondered if Theo was just as invested in Good Vibes as she was. "We put together a great selection of toys and all kinds of rainbow accessories to fill up the display window. Libby put the purchase order in right before we went to Vegas."

Libby's mouth dropped open.

"Sweetie?"

"Shit."

"What's wrong?"

"The freaking purchase order!" Libby smacked her forehead. "I knew I was forgetting something before we left. I thought it was something I was supposed to pack, but when I never needed it, I figured it wasn't important. Shit, shit, shit!"

"Is it too late?" her mom asked. "You can submit the purchase order when you get home tonight."

"No, it's too late" Libby said with a heavy sigh. "It

would never get processed in time. I'd be lucky to get my shipment by the end of June. Damn it." She'd done it *again*. "What are we going to put in the display window for Pride now?"

Both Theo and her mom were looking at her with sad puppy dog eyes, a mix of pity and disappointment that Libby knew all too well.

"I told you, I'm no good at planning."

Her mom sighed. She set down her slice of pizza. "Sweetie, I say this with love, but that's bullshit."

Libby blinked. "What?"

"I know exactly what you're capable of," her mom said. "When you were a kid and you decided you wanted to learn how to sew, you were unstoppable. You got so good at it in just a few months. I was so impressed and proud of you. And when you decided to open your shop, how many people told you it was a crazy risk?"

"A lot."

"But you did it anyway because it was important to you. And it might have taken a few years to get your footing, but you're doing so well now," her mom said. "You're not bad at planning but you are kind of bad at taking responsibility. You can't just focus on the parts of the business that are the most fun. You have to own the whole process."

Libby glanced at Theo. It was never fun getting chewed out by your mom, and even less fun when you had an audience. Theo gave her a sympathetic look but Libby could tell she agreed.

Her mom got up and held out her hand for their plates. "Everybody done?"

Libby handed hers over with a slice of untouched pizza still on it. Suddenly, she wasn't so hungry anymore.

When Libby and Theo got back to her apartment, Libby kept herself busy, digging her sewing machine out of the back of her closet. She set it up on the little folding card table that served as her dining table and while she was dusting it off and rethreading it, Theo leaned against the kitchen counter and watched.

"What are you going to do with the dress?"

"I'm thinking it'll make a nice tutu," Libby said. "I'll take it apart first, salvage as much tulle as I can, then dye each piece a different color and stitch it all back together in rainbow layers."

"Sounds really cool," Theo said. "I would never have the patience to do all that."

"I don't know about that. You *do* have the patience to come up with complex rules for your game," Libby pointed out, eager to latch onto a subject that was not Good Vibes. "How's that going, by the way?"

"I haven't worked on it in a while," Theo admitted. "Don't see much point when it'll just end up shelved beside all the other games in my bedroom."

"It doesn't have to," Libby said, laying the Victorian dress on the floor and sitting down to take a pair of fabric shears to it. "Why don't you look into getting an exhibitor booth at SexyCon next year? Even if you don't have a manufacturer and the whole nine yards, you could show people how the game is played and gauge their interest, like market research. Start driving traffic to a mailing list so you've got customers when you're ready to launch."

Theo grinned. "Don't look now, but you're talking like a businesswoman who knows what she's doing."

Libby rolled her eyes. "Apparently not."

She cut the bodice off her old costume. No amount of creative tailoring would make the top half of that dress fit a grown woman with curves like Libby's, but the skirt was still totally usable. She tossed the bodice toward the trash can and paused before her next cut.

"Do you think my mom was right?"

"I feel like that question is a landmine."

"I just want honest feedback," Libby said. She held up three fingers. "Scout's honor."

Theo laughed. "You're not a Scout."

"The sentiment holds."

Theo thought for a minute, then she joined Libby on the floor. "Honestly? I think she's right that you use spontaneity as a crutch sometimes. If you don't take anything seriously, you can't take it personally if it doesn't work out."

"Ouch."

"Sorry."

"No," Libby sighed. "You're right. It just sucks hearing it out loud."

"Do you want to wear my clothes for a while?" Theo

teased. "You can channel my analytical side and we can work through some alternative Pride plans."

Libby laughed. "Thanks, but I'd rather keep working on this tutu for now. Will you talk to me while I sew?"

"Of course."

She finished cutting the skirt, laying the layers of tulle out in big, flat squares on her apartment floor, and while she worked, she and Theo wound up brainstorming everything they could do to promote Good Vibes on short notice.

By the time Libby stood in front of her mirror, a rainbow-colored tutu around her waist and Theo by her side, they had a plan she felt good about.

"You're amazing, you know that?"

"I know," Theo joked. "But so are you. You've got a lot of fight in you and I really admire that."

"So," Libby said, narrowing her eyes and looking Theo up and down. "Only one question remains."

"Which is?"

"What are *you* wearing to Pride?"

"A Good Vibes t-shirt, of course."

17

THEO

"You might not think you've got a mind for planning, but you definitely make up for it with enthusiasm," Theo said as she came up behind Libby and wrapped her in her arms.

They were in Libby's living room again, standing in the middle of a huge pile of rainbow tutus that Libby had managed to sew in just one short week. She was wearing the prototype she'd made out of her old Victorian costume and she looked positively radiant.

"These are really easy to make," she said, holding up another tutu. "A little bit of tulle in rainbow colors, an elastic band and a couple minutes on the sewing machine – nothing to them."

Theo knew exactly what had gone into making the fifty tutus filling every nook and cranny of Libby's small apartment – Theo had done a lot of the cutting and pinning prep work, following Libby's careful instructions.

"What are you going to sell them for?"

"I don't know," Libby said, cocking her head adorably to the side as she considered. "Cheap materials, fast to make... fifteen bucks?"

"What?" Theo gaped. "These are thirty-five-dollar tutus, minimum."

Libby pushed back. "But just picture the store windows completely filled with rainbow tutus and a big sign telling people they're only fifteen dollars. Who could pass up a fifteen-dollar tutu on their way to Pride? They'll sell out in twenty minutes and I'll have fifty new customers."

"I love you."

Libby giggled. "I love you, too, but what does that have to do with this?"

"We really need to work on building your business confidence because you're way more strategic than you let on," Theo said. "That's a really great idea. You know what else these tutus need?"

"What?"

"The Good Vibes logo embroidered on the outside of every waistband," Theo said. "That way no one will mistake where they came from."

"Free promotion - smart," Libby said. "I'll have to find a seamstress who can do the job on extremely short notice-"

"Let me take care of it," Theo said. "You just work on making your window display as eye-catching as possible."

Libby narrowed her eyes at Theo. "You wouldn't be trying to procrastinate, would you?"

Theo gave her an innocent shrug. "I don't know what you're talking about."

"Your game," Libby answered. She twisted out of Theo's grasp and put her hands on her hips. "You promised you'd work on it and instead, you spent every free minute of the last week helping me with the tutus."

"That was the priority," Theo said. "Pride Month starts in a week but SexyCon isn't for a couple more months."

"I'm not going to let you shove your dreams aside because you're too busy helping me with mine," Libby said. She shimmied out of her tutu, leaving her in a pair of athletic shorts and a vintage band t-shirt. It was, quite possibly, the least flamboyant thing she'd ever let Theo see her in, with the exception of her pajamas. "You said you have ideas for a few new cards, right?"

Theo nodded.

"And Andie's out of town visiting Robin," Libby added with a smirk. "Who knew those two would hit it off so fast?" She looped her arms around Theo's neck, looking into her eyes with the seductive gaze she knew would turn Theo to putty in her hands. "So take me back to your place and I'll help you test those cards. We've spent enough time on tutus for one day."

"You don't have to tell me twice," Theo said, pulling her toward the door.

"Ooh, I got the *thighs* card. One of my favorites," Libby said, setting it on the bed between them with a wink. Theo's game was still in its 'hand-written on index cards' stage and they'd played it so many times that all but her most recent additions to the deck were dog-eared.

She shuffled through the three Action cards in her hand. *Nibble* and *lick* were early additions – obvious choices for a game that had been inspired by a pair of sex dice. But she'd also drawn one of her new cards and she couldn't wait to play it.

"*Spank*," Libby read with a grin. "Okay, I like it... but let's spice things up a bit more, shall we?"

She played a Heat card from her hand, denoted by a hastily scribbled flame Theo had drawn on the back of each Heat card. Theo read it aloud as Libby set it down. "*Supplement this round with a toy of the player's choosing.*"

Libby got up and retrieved a riding crop from the toy box she'd brought over to Theo's place when they first started developing the game. She handed it to Theo and sat down on the bed again, propping herself on her elbows.

Theo set her remaining cards face-down and started the timer on her phone. She got to her knees, slapping the riding crop once her palm. "How hard?"

"You're the one holding the riding crop," Libby said, hardly able to contain her excitement. "That's for you to decide."

Theo used the leather loop to nudge Libby's knees apart, enjoying the sight of her smooth, creamy thighs.

"Hurry," Libby said. "Time's a wasting-"

The word was cut off abruptly in her mouth as Theo snapped the riding crop against her thigh. "Too hard?"

"Don't apologize. Just do it again, babe."

Theo obliged. She teased the riding crop up and down Libby's thighs, giving her lighter and sharper smacks as she went. When she moved the crop higher up Libby's legs, sliding over the crotch of her shorts, Libby shivered and the timer went off.

Theo pulled the crop away and Libby sat up, breathing a little heavier. "We're going to have to make a rule about what happens when you cheat."

"I didn't cheat."

"The card was *thighs,* not *pussy,*" Libby pointed out. "There needs to be a punishment card."

"Noted," Theo said.

"Your turn, babe. I like the new cards, by the way."

Theo gave her a mischievous grin, then picked her cards up again. She thought for a minute before laying down *back*.

Libby chose *massage* to go with it and Theo used a Heat card to extend her time. She lay down on her stomach and Libby straddled Theo's hips, her hands sliding under her shirt to knead her muscles.

"Mm, that feels good."

"Yeah, it does," Libby agreed, her hips moving along with her hands. They'd been playing for about fifteen minutes and had already gone through half a dozen rounds. Twenty minutes was their record – the longest they'd ever made it without one of them cracking under the building pressure and losing in the best possible way – with an orgasm. By the way Libby was grinding her hips against Theo's ass, she could tell today wouldn't be a record-breaker.

If Libby came right now, Theo would get to play her Fantasy card – a fill-in-the-blank one that changed with every game and guaranteed things would never get boring. This time, she'd written *Eat me in front of the full-length mirror so I can watch.*

The very idea made her throb with desire and Libby let out a little moan that told Theo she was getting closer to her wish. The timer went off and Theo said, "We still don't have a rule for cheaters, right?"

"Not unless you made one up in the last two minutes."

"Good." She spun around and grabbed Libby, pulling her down to the bed with a startled giggle. Theo had her pinned, wrinkling a few more cards in the process as she kissed her and shoved her hand down Libby's shorts.

"Not fair!" Her mouth protested but her body rose to seek Theo's hand. She spread her thighs and Theo slipped her fingers through Libby's folds.

"You're so wet."

"I'm so close." She barely got the sentence out before Theo found her clit, running her finger over it in the tight circles she knew Libby loved. Libby reached for her, too, but Theo kept her pinned, a grin on her lips.

"Game master's prerogative," she said. "I get to invoke God Mode from time to time."

She yanked Libby's shorts down and reached for the

riding crop again, giving her thighs a couple more swift smacks before she brought her mouth down to Libby's intoxicating nectar. Libby was squirming and moaning in no time, threading her fingers through Theo's hair and screaming as Theo brought her to the edge.

Libby clamped her thighs around Theo's head, her whole body shaking as she came, and when she finally collapsed, satisfied, Theo looked at her from between Libby's legs. With a smile, she said, "You lose."

"Only because you're a big, fat cheater," Libby said. "I demand a punishment card be added to the deck before we play again."

"Did you really hate losing that much?"

"On principle, yes," Libby said, sitting up and snatching Theo's Fantasy card, written on a yellow index card to set it apart. Libby read it, grinned, then got out of the bed and pulled Theo by the hand. "Come on, claim your prize."

A little shiver of excitement worked its way down Theo's spine and into her belly as she followed Libby down the hall to stand in front of the full-length bathroom mirror.

She'd never thought of herself as adventurous before she met Libby. Things tended to stay in the bedroom and she never strayed far from her sexual comfort zone. It was so different with Libby, though. She made Theo want to push her limits. She made her ravenous and eager to please, and there was something so satisfying about watching Libby kneel before her to taste her.

Libby padded barefoot into the bathroom and Theo

closed the door behind her, revealing the full-length mirror she'd been fantasizing about. Another little shiver made Theo's stomach quiver.

That was the other thing about Libby – every time Theo had been aware of how her stomach felt in the last couple of years, it was because she felt bad. Nerves equaled stomach ache, and stomach ache equaled panic. But lately, those nerves felt a lot more like butterflies and the sensation tended to be lower than before, a tingling in her core that she didn't mind at all.

The only conclusion Theo could draw was that their great big, scary excursion to Vegas had cured her. *Libby* had cured her.

She walked Theo backward until her heels hit the edge of the bathtub. She stumbled a little but Libby wrapped her arms around Theo and steadied her. Then she dropped to her knees. Theo followed her with her eyes as Libby unbuttoned her pants.

"Look in the mirror, silly," she said.

"Okay." Theo watched Libby do a slow, teasing job of pulling her pants down and noticed a problem with her fantasy. "You're wearing way too many clothes, babe."

"Just my t-shirt," Libby said.

"Exactly."

Theo sat on the edge of the tub and pulled Libby's shirt over her head. She was already braless and Theo cupped her breasts in her hands, kissing Libby as the nervous, excited sensation built between her legs.

"Eat me – please," she whispered at last.

Libby obediently bowed her head. Theo spread her

legs wide and gathered Libby's teal hair in one fist. The way her head bobbed and her perfectly round ass bounced against her heels as she lapped at Theo, along with the echo of their combined moans in the small, tiled room, all harmonized to bring Theo to the edge pretty quickly.

She saw Libby move her hand in the mirror, then she felt Libby's palm on her leg. It was a surreal feeling, anticipating her touches before they happened. Libby glided her hand slowly up Theo's leg, over her knee and along the inside of her thigh.

By the time she found Theo's folds, Theo had shifted her hips to the edge of the tub and she was ready for her. Libby thrust her fingers inside her, tongue never stopping its motions over her clit, and Theo threw back her head to groan at the ceiling.

It didn't take much.

She was already so riled up from the game, and from making Libby come hard against her mouth. Theo came quickly, with her body clenching around Libby's fingers and her hips seeking Libby's mouth.

She nearly lost her balance and fell into the tub. They both laughed as she braced herself against the opposite edge and rode out the receding waves of her orgasm.

"I think that was a pretty successful round of the game," Libby said, a satisfied smirk on her face. "How much more practice do you need before you feel confident enough to start showing it to other people?"

"At least a hundred more games," Theo teased,

pulling Libby into her lap on the edge of the tub. "In fact, I could play another round right now."

"Could you?"

"Mm hmm."

"Well, I told you I'm your number one product tester," Libby said, kissing Theo and pulling her to her feet. "If you say it needs another round of testing then damn it, we're going to do that testing!"

They left their clothes in a pile on the bathroom floor and went into the hallway, but Theo pulled Libby left instead of right. "We've been working hard – I think we deserve a break to rehydrate, maybe order some food."

"Good thinking."

Theo went to the fridge and handed Libby a beer. "The game needs at least one more thing before we can share it."

"What's that?"

"A name."

She took a long, cold sip and enjoyed the freedom of drinking a cold one in the buff, her body still pulsing from her orgasm. Then the front door swung open and Theo locked eyes with Andie.

"Stark-naked lesbians!" Andie said. "Oh my!"

Theo ducked behind the kitchen island and Libby just laughed. "That's actually not a bad name!"

18

LIBBY

"What are you doing back already?" Theo asked Andie. She grabbed a floral kitchen towel off the oven handle and passed it to Libby, who couldn't decide whether to drape it across her chest or hold it up in front of herself like an awkward, sunflower-decorated sensor bar. "I thought you and Robin were spending the whole weekend together."

They'd been getting more and more cozy, talking via text messages and video chats, and Libby had done everything she could to encourage the relationship. What was more romantic than having your best friend fall for your girlfriend's best friend?

She was already seeing double dates and couples' vacations in their future, but then Andie came in and tossed her overnight bag on the floor with a sigh.

"We were supposed to," she said, draping herself across the couch as if Theo and Libby weren't desperately attempting to conceal their nakedness.

Or at least, Theo was. Libby was being modest for her girlfriend's sake, but she didn't particularly care whether Andie got an eyeful or not. She knew Andie wasn't interested in her and they'd already spent a whole weekend sharing a bathroom in Vegas. Why bother with false modesty?

"What happened?" she asked.

"I fucked it up," Andie said with a shrug. "I told you we were going to the Nat Butler concert because Robin had never seen her live before, right?"

"Yeah." Theo was still looking around for a matching kitchen towel, or anything else that might provide some coverage. Libby snorted when she settled on an oven mitt across her chest and a pot holder in front of her crotch.

"Well, when I got to Toronto, Robin surprised me with backstage passes," Andie continued.

"Aww, that's so sweet," Libby crooned, nearly dropping her towel as she started to clasp her hands in front of her chest and then thought better of it. "Last time I talked to Robin, she told me she really likes you."

"Maybe she *did,*" Andie answered. "Before this weekend."

"Oh no, what did you do?" Theo asked.

"Well, the concert was great. We had amazing seats and Nat played all her greatest hits," Andie said. "Then we got backstage. The meet-and-greet line was enormous, and Nat Butler actually ended up walking right past us to get to her dressing room. *And* she recognized me from the concert last year."

"That's pretty cool," Theo said.

"She must really care about her fans," Libby added.

"I thought it was cool, too," Andie said, a bashful tone coming into her voice.

Theo asked again, "What did you do?"

"I *may* have accidentally tripped Robin in my hurry to say hi to Nat," Andie said, not meeting either of their eyes. "And *maybe* I didn't notice until after Nat left and I turned around to see Robin glaring at me from the ground while some other woman helped her up."

"Shit."

"Yeah, she ended up scraping her hands on the concrete," Andie said. "She might have gotten over the fact that I basically forgot she existed for a minute when Nat was there if only I'd offered to take her home right away. But we still had backstage passes..."

"Oh, Andie."

"I know, not my finest hour. Nat Butler makes me do crazy things."

"No, you do crazy things because you're ridiculous," Theo said.

"I'm not the one holding a pot holder in front of my bush right now." Andie pointed out.

"I'm sure Robin will forgive you," Libby said. "She's probably already laughing about it."

"I don't know about that," Andie said. "At the very least, I soured her on Nat Butler forever. Hey, you two look like you could use a third wheel for Penny's wedding."

Theo gave her a sympathetic look. "Did your

weekend trip really go *that* badly? I thought you already invited Robin."

"I don't think she's going to be over this ordeal by the end of the month. Guess I'm flying solo."

"You're always welcome to tag along with us," Libby said. "It's the least I could do in return for you and Penny inviting me along on the Vegas trip."

"Great," Theo said. "Now that's settled and we can trade our kitchen accessories for actual clothes."

She nudged Libby around the island, following behind her to cover her backside as much as she could. As they headed down the hall to Theo's room, Andie said, "Hey, you're going to wash that pot holder, right? Plus whatever other surfaces the two of you desecrated while I was gone?"

"If you're concerned about that, I wouldn't sit on the couch," Libby called over her shoulder with a snort.

Theo went back to the end of the hall, peeking around the corner to find Andie looking disgustedly at the couch cushions and said, "We didn't actually do it on the couch."

With plenty of help from Theo, Josie and Libby's mom, Good Vibes got a complete rainbow transformation just in time for Pride in the East Village.

Libby's vision for a front window display entirely out of rainbow tutus was realized, complete with embroidered logos, and she came by the shop with Theo on the morning of the Pride Festival to give it a final once-over. As they stood on the sidewalk admiring the floor to ceiling rainbow of tulle, Libby took Theo's hand. "What do you think?"

"I think it looks fantastic," she said. "And I think it would be a pretty darn good effort regardless of how long ago you started planning. It's impressive."

"Thank you," Libby said as a couple of revelers walked past on their way to the party. She smiled as she watched their heads turn automatically to her display. "Come on, babe, let's open the shop."

They went inside and Libby manned the register for about an hour while she waited for her mom to arrive. She sold three tutus off the wall and Josie stopped in wearing a Good Vibes t-shirt along with a skirt in the pink, yellow and blue colors of the pansexual flag.

"The shop looks great," she said. "I'm going to predict you sell out of tutus by noon."

"I hope so," Libby said. "Hey, I gave you the day off so you could have fun at Pride. What are you doing here?"

"I'm going, I'm going," Josie laughed. "See you there."

She left and Libby sold one more tutu to a girl who looked to be about fifteen and shy. She visibly brightened the moment she pulled the tutu over her waist and there was a little more bounce in her step as she walked out the door.

"*That's* why I wanted to sell them for fifteen dollars," Libby said, beaming as she watched the girl disappear into the gathering crowd on the sidewalk. "Theo, thank you so much for all your help this year. I don't know where I'd be without you, but it sure as hell wouldn't be as good as all this."

"This is all your hard work," Theo said. "Don't forget it."

"It's on account of your guidance, though," Libby insisted as the door chimed and her mom came in. She was wearing a white shirt with the word *Ally* printed on it in rainbow colors, plus suspenders with a variety of enamel pins that Libby had loaned her for the occasion, including her collection of pride flags she'd gathered over the years. "Looking good, Mom."

"As do you – both of you," she said.

Libby stepped out from behind the counter and did a little twirl. Her prototype skirt had more of a tie-dyed effect than the tutus she was selling in the window and the tulle was a little longer, flowing as she spun. She'd dyed her hair blonde and braided a rainbow of different yarns into her ponytail. Even her heels had rainbow shades of glitter glued to them.

Theo had been skeptical of that, asking why Libby would want to walk around in heels all day long, to which Libby had simply replied that sometimes, beauty required sacrifice.

"Not for me," Theo had retorted, so Libby bought a pair of canvas sneakers to glitter up for Theo, and made her a tie-dyed pair of board shorts that matched Libby's skirt.

"No tutu for you, Theo?" Libby's mom asked.

"Not on my life," she said with a chuckle. "But Libby

looks great in hers. I knew she sewed, but I had no idea she was such a talented seamstress. She's practically a one-woman textile factory."

"She *is* good, isn't she?" her mom said. "Well, let me take over so you two can enjoy yourselves. Anything I need to know?"

"Tutus are fifteen dollars, everything else is ten percent off," Libby said. She gave her mom a hug, then took Theo's hand. "Thanks for watching the shop so Josie and I can both have the day off."

"My pleasure, sweetie."

East Village Pride was five blocks long and already pretty crowded by the time Libby and Theo arrived around ten in the morning. More people would keep pouring into the space as the day went on, especially once the stage shows began at noon. For now, people were mostly just wandering around, getting their bearings and saying hello to familiar faces.

Libby and Theo found Josie getting a frozen lemonade from one of the food trucks parked all around the perimeter of the festival, and Theo bought Libby a breakfast funnel cake because, as Libby put it, "Pride only comes once a year, so why not have powdered sugar and fried dough for breakfast?"

They wandered for a while and as soon as she polished off her funnel cake, Libby looped her arm in Theo's. Going to a Pride festival with someone was an entirely new experience – she'd been to dozens of them with her mom, with Robin, with groups of people she loosely called friends. But she'd never proudly walked down the street, hand linked with a woman she loved, as the whole block swelled to bursting with gay pride.

The sensation was without comparison, certainly without words, and she stopped to kiss Theo at least a dozen times just because she could.

By the time the bands started playing at noon, Libby was drunk with love and pride and a fierce possessiveness not just for Theo, but for every stranger that passed her – especially the ones wearing familiar rainbow tutus.

These were her people, even more than the SexyCon crowd, and she'd never *really* felt such a deep sense of belonging before.

Now, thanks to Theo, she did.

"Yes! The Scarlet Begonias are playing," Libby said, dragging Theo over to the stage where one of her favorite indie bands was setting up.

The area was filling up fast and they had to squeeze into the throng of people just to get a good view. Theo stood behind Libby and wrapped her arms around her, looking over her head as the band launched into their first song.

Libby tilted her head back to look at her. "You doing okay?"

It wasn't quite as chaotic as Vegas had been, or as strange as SexyCon, but Pride could be a lot to handle and Libby had seen Theo thrown off by much less.

"I'm great," she said, kissing Libby's forehead. "I love you."

"I love you, too," Libby said, her chest swelling once again and syncing with the music this time.

Andie found the two of them after a while, attached at the hip to a pretty redhead Libby and Theo had never seen before and, in Libby's estimation, trying a little *too* hard to pretend she didn't care that it wasn't Robin.

They bumped into Josie again later when they were perusing the vendor tables, and by the end of the afternoon, Libby was exhausted and entirely unable to wipe the smile off her face.

They meandered back up the street in the direction of Good Vibes and Libby's apartment once the festivities ended. Her mom had already closed up shop. The windows were dark and the sun had set long ago, but Libby could see that there was not a single tutu left in the display.

"Congratulations," Theo said, scooping Libby up in a proud hug. "You totally rocked Pride this year."

Libby grinned a little wider and when Theo set her back on her feet, she blurted, "Move in with me."

"What?"

"Move in with me," she repeated. "How many nights have we spent apart lately? Hardly any, and just imagine the fortune we'd save on toothbrushes if we didn't both have extra ones at each other's places."

Theo laughed, but Libby could see a storm brewing in her blue-gray eyes.

"Or not," Libby hedged. "It was just a thought-"

"I like the idea," Theo said. Lie – obviously a lie. Libby could see it in her eyes. "But what about Andie? Rent's expensive and I can't just ditch her."

"Okay, that's a fair point-"

"I think I need to go home."

It was abrupt, like a curtain falling over Theo's previously good mood. It made Libby want to stagger back, but instead she took Theo's hand because it looked like she was about to make a sprint for the subway.

"Wait," she said, forcing her voice to be calm. She'd gotten good at reading Theo's panic signals – the false calm that hid a racing pulse, eyes that darted around, looking for an escape. "We don't have to talk about that right now, but I still want you to stay the night with me like we planned. You said you didn't want to worry about crowded subways tonight, remember?"

"I'm sorry," Theo said. Her eyes were wild now and Libby let go of her hand, knowing the gesture probably made her feel trapped. "It's not the moving in together thing – it was the crowds today. All that noise, so many people... my nerves are frayed."

Another lie – Theo had been fine all day. Libby knew that because she'd been subtly monitoring her, making sure she was okay.

"We'll go back to your place tonight, then," Libby suggested. "Let me just run upstairs and grab a change of clothes-"

"I can't wait," Theo said. "I'm sorry, I have to go *now*."

"Theo," Libby objected, but her girlfriend was already backing away from her as if *she* was the monster no one else could see.

Libby's heart twisted in her chest. Why did she have to blurt out that stupid idea?

It was a stupid idea that had been rolling around in her head for a while. A stupid idea she thought Theo would be excited about, but that she obviously shouldn't have brought up so casually.

A stupid idea that suddenly had her on the verge of tears.

Theo was already halfway down the block by the time Libby called, her voice so low she wasn't even sure Theo heard, "Don't shut me out. Please."

Theo turned around at the corner of the block and called, "I just need to go home right now. I'm sorry. I'll call you first thing in the morning, okay?"

Libby could hear the panic, unmistakable in Theo's voice. So she let her go, and when Theo disappeared, Libby slid down the wall outside Good Vibes, landing in a heap of crumpled tulle in the doorway.

She watched rainbow-dressed people pass by on their way to the subway and none of them even noticed her in the shadows of the shop entrance. A few of them wore her tutus and they were all smiling, all still illuminated with that incredible Pride glow.

Suddenly, Libby didn't feel any of that anymore.

All she felt was abandoned, like she'd said the wrong thing and Theo couldn't wait to get away from her. It was a pretty familiar feeling, just like high school.

She took out her phone and typed out a text to Theo, her eyes blurred with tears.

I don't want you to feel trapped by the idea of moving in together. You could still escape whenever you wanted.

She hit send, swiped angrily at the tears staining her cheeks, then sent another quick message.

My dad sure did.

Libby regretted that second message immediately, but she couldn't take it back. She cringed as she watched the delivery notification appear, putting the phone away before it could turn from 'delivered' to 'read'.

Then she dragged herself upstairs to her apartment and flopped into bed, tutu and all.

19

THEO

Theo had just reached the subway platform when she felt her phone vibrating in her pocket. Her thoughts were still racing, begging her to go as fast as her feet could take her back to the safety of her apartment. But the train hadn't arrived yet so she stepped out of the flow of foot traffic to read Libby's message. It knocked the wind out of her.

My dad sure did.

Theo read the whole message several times over. Her stomach was still twisting with panic but this made her heart ache, too.

"Oh, Libby."

Even as she stood outside of Good Vibes and felt the panic building, Theo hated what she was doing to Libby. She could see the whole conversation from outside her body and it was ugly.

Theo was being petty and mean, allowing her anxiety to overwhelm her rather than just being honest with

Libby and telling her that the thought of moving in together scared the hell out of her. It wasn't Libby – Theo loved her more than she thought possible.

It was the possibility of linking their lives, then letting her anxiety drag them both down. Theo couldn't do that to Libby, but she also couldn't find the words to explain it while the panic overtook her brain.

The worst part was that she was completely aware of her actions. She knew she wasn't sick. There was no danger, no invisible monsters. But even as her mind recoiled from her actions, her body kept compelling her forward to the lie of safety at home.

The train arrived and people started moving toward the doors, the subway platform churning with traffic.

Get on that train, Theo's anxiety told her. *Do it now before something bad happens.*

No.

She couldn't just leave Libby to think she was being abandoned all over again. She loved her, and you don't do that to people you love. That was the real 'something bad' that would happen.

Any minute now, Theo's anxiety continued to taunt her, along with the racing of her pulse. *Tick, tick, tick… what if you pass out and everyone just leaves you there? What if you fall onto the tracks and another train comes? What if-*

"Shut up," Theo grumbled, turning a few heads.

Great. Now she was one of those lunatics that talks to themselves on the subway and scares the people around them.

"Sorry," she said to a woman hurrying past with a child in her arms. The apology didn't seem to help and it did nothing to stop the panicked voices inside Theo's head.

What if you lose control?

Theo swallowed hard as that thought sent a fresh bolt of panic through her. She started pacing back and forth on the subway platform, giving up on the calm façade and even giving up on the whole *not talking to herself* thing.

"I'm okay," she mumbled under her breath. "I feel sick but it's just my anxiety playing a trick on me." Those words came courtesy of her therapist – it was a mantra she'd been trying to train Theo to say. "If something bad is going to happen, it doesn't matter whether I'm here or in my apartment, or at Libby's place. One is not inherently safer than the others."

That part of the mantra was courtesy of Libby, and the rational part of Theo's brain agreed with her. It was just too bad her agoraphobia resided in an entirely irrational part of her mind.

Passengers piled onto the train and the doors slid shut with Theo still pacing on the platform. She watched the train disappear into the tunnel and her heart was still pounding just as hard as ever, but she'd made her choice and now she was stuck for better or worse - her escape vehicle had just pulled away.

Theo took a deep breath, then went back up to the street. Her anxiety medicine was in a drawer in her desk at home, doing her exactly zero good, but she just kept thinking of Libby and how awful she must be feeling. For the first time in three years, Theo was determined to live her life in spite of the panic attack.

She wasn't going to run out of a convention center gasping for air, or hole up in a hotel bathroom, or let her fears ruin another relationship.

This one was too important.

Good Vibes was still dark and locked up tight when Theo got back to it, and the apartment above was dark, too. Theo rang the bell and called Libby's phone but got no answer, and she sent her a couple of texts that went unread.

Hey, I'm downstairs.
I'm really sorry I left.

She got no response and Theo wondered if Libby had gone back out, perhaps to one of the bars on the block where the Pride party continued?

A new layer of dread settled in Theo's stomach at the idea of walking from bar to crowded bar looking for Libby. But first, she'd try something else.

"Libby?" Theo called up to the apartment. She stepped off the curb and cupped her hands around her mouth to call her girlfriend's name again. "Libby! I'm so sorry I left!"

There was still no answer, but Theo saw movement from Libby's bedroom. She was home and ignoring her, and Theo deserved that.

"Can you hear me?" Theo called up. "I'm not going anywhere, okay? I won't leave you." She waited a minute and saw more movement from the bedroom, but Libby didn't come to the window. Out of options, Theo eyed the fire escape, then decided it had to be done. "Fine. If you won't come down, I'm coming up to you."

The fire escape looked old and rusty and Theo's stomach felt like she'd swallowed a large stone but she'd had enough cowardice for one night. She made a running leap and grabbed the lowest rung of the ladder, pulling it down.

It made an awful, rusty racket and she was lucky there weren't many people walking down the street at that moment. Otherwise, she might have been dealing with the police on top of a panic attack and an injured girlfriend.

Theo climbed the ladder to the platform outside Libby's bedroom window, and the whole thing shook as Theo navigated it. Her heart was still racing, but now the very real fear of falling to her death had overwhelmed the irrational panic.

Libby opened her window as soon as Theo reached it and asked, "What the hell are you doing?"

"You wouldn't answer your phone," Theo said. "I had to tell you that I'm sorry I freaked out and left."

"So you climbed up my fire escape?"

"Yes."

Libby sighed and for a minute, Theo wondered whether she'd send her right back down the way she'd come. But then Libby moved aside. "Get in here before you hurt yourself."

Theo climbed through the window and Libby shut it, then turned on a bedside lamp. She was still wearing the rainbow yarn in her hair, now frizzy from her pillow, and her eyeliner was smeared.

"Have you been crying?" Theo asked. Libby nodded, but then she allowed Theo to scoop her into her arms. "I'm sorry I ruined Pride."

"You didn't ruin it," Libby said, her words muffled against Theo's t-shirt. "I never should have sprung that idea on you. I got caught up in the moment – it was a stupid idea."

"No, it really wasn't. I just wish I'd responded better."

Libby was quiet for a minute, then she looked up at Theo. "Does that mean the answer is still no?"

Theo sighed. "It's not because of you. You're the most amazing person I've ever met. I'm constantly in awe of you and I love you-"

"How could it not be me?" Libby asked. Almost inaudibly, she added, "What's wrong with me?"

"*Nothing*," Theo said, holding her even tighter. "Not a damn thing, and I'm not your father."

She felt Libby stiffen against her and wondered if she'd crossed a line. She murmured into Theo's chest, "I shouldn't have sent that text."

"You were speaking from the heart," Theo said. "I'm so sorry that you didn't get the kind of unconditional love from your dad that you deserved."

Theo pulled Libby back so she could look into her eyes. Tears clung to her eyelashes and her lower lip quivered. The sight broke Theo's heart, and it also sent a surge of anger through her. Libby didn't deserve a dad who was that selfish, and she deserved better than she got from Theo tonight, too.

"I need to tell you something from my heart now," Theo said. "When we met, I was using my anxiety as a shield to protect me from getting close to people. I turned my agoraphobia into a weapon and I used it to push my ex-girlfriend away until she just gave up on me. And then I kept on using it to shelter myself from everything new and scary in life. Until you came along. You made me want to try again."

"And you're doing really well," Libby said. "Look at everything we've done in the past year. SexyCon, Vegas, Pride – even that Franz Erhard Walther exhibit was kind of off the wall."

"That's my point," Theo said. "I'm doing well right now but anxiety is a constant battle and I can't predict when I'm going to backslide. You're so adventurous and free-spirited, I never want to hold you back. If we lived together and my world started to constrict again for whatever reason, I don't think I could bear it if I held you back and you started to resent me for it."

"I would never resent you," Libby said. "Do you love me?"

"More than anything," Theo said. "So much it hurts sometimes."

"And you're *in love* with me?"

"Head over heels. I love you so much, Libby."

"I love you, too," she said, wrapping her arms around Theo. "And I'm not going anywhere, either. No matter how much you try to push me away. We'll keep our current living arrangement for now and we can revisit the idea when we're both ready for that next step."

"Thank you," Theo said. "I do want to move in with you eventually, babe. And I wasn't just using Andie as an excuse earlier – we'll have to keep her in the loop because New York rents are insane."

Libby laughed. "We can do that." She pulled back and looked into Theo's eyes. "Just promise you won't shut me out again. We can't work through things if we don't talk."

"That's why I came back tonight," Theo said. "I promise I won't make that mistake again."

Libby kissed her and Theo tasted a faint saltiness on her lips. She still hated that she'd made Libby cry and now that the panic had subsided, she was determined to make it up to her.

"Are we okay?" she asked.

"We're perfect."

"Good," Theo said. "Then lay back. We need to end Pride with a bang."

Libby laughed as Theo tossed the hem of her rainbow tutu in the air, then dove beneath the layers of tulle.

20

LIBBY

Penny's wedding was at a vineyard with a beautiful view of Hemlock Lake. She and Chet were married at sunset on a dock right over the water, the setting sun reflecting across the lake and perfectly matching their salmon and gray wedding colors.

It was such a well-coordinated moment that Libby wouldn't have been surprised to find out Penny had come out here with fabric swatches to color-match the sky.

During the ceremony, Theo stood beside Penny as her maid of honor, and as far as Libby was concerned, she stole the spotlight in a handsome, light gray suit and salmon-colored tie. Every time she made discrete eye contact with Libby sitting in the third row, her heart swelled with pride.

That's my *girlfriend,* she thought each time their eyes met. *All mine.*

That proud sensation had been overtaking her a lot lately, ever since the night of Pride when they'd made that promise to each other. *I won't leave you – I'm not going anywhere.* They were just words, but Libby could see in Theo's eyes that she meant them with all her heart.

"You can't cry before the bride does." Robin leaned over in the seat beside Libby to whisper to her.

"Huh?" Libby whispered back.

"I see you tearing up," Robin teased. "It's an unspoken rule – no crying if the bride isn't crying."

"Whatever," Libby said with a sniff. "Like I'm going to take wedding etiquette advice from a big sap like you."

"Who's a sap?" Robin asked.

"Shh," Libby's mom shushed them both from her seat on Libby's other side. They hushed like little kids being scolded – old habits die hard – and Libby gave Robin a conspiratorial smile.

She was wearing an A-line skirt and blouse from H&M that flattered her curvy figure. It was far more structured and sophisticated than anything she would have worn when they were younger, but it really suited her.

Robin had changed a lot over the years. At first, Libby felt left behind, then she'd felt rejected, but their friendship managed to weather all the growing pains and now she just felt proud of her friend.

The Robin that Libby had known over the Internet in high school never would have had the confidence to reach out and patch things up with Andie. She'd been shy and uncertain back then, wearing her cat ears like a shield to protect herself.

She'd shed her eclectic style while Libby held onto

her own, but they'd both done a whole hell of a lot of growing up in the intervening years. And here they were, both smiling up at their women standing on the dock.

Libby caught Andie, in a salmon-colored tea dress, beaming back at Robin from her place next to Theo. They'd all found love and happiness, and this whole day was about celebrating that fact. Libby's heart had never felt fuller.

What a crazy, constantly evolving world.

Penny and Chet exchanged vows they'd written themselves. Penny teared up and so did Libby, dabbing her eyes with a vintage handkerchief. Then Chet lightened the mood with a few laughs he'd built into his vows.

As they said their *I dos* and exchanged rings, Libby kept her eyes on Theo. God, she was an amazing woman, far stronger than she realized and forever surprising Libby. It hadn't taken long at all for Theo to usurp Robin, and even her mom, as Libby's favorite human.

And that didn't even touch on how unbelievably sexy she was...

Libby and Theo had arrived at the vineyard hours before the ceremony so Theo could help her sister get ready. Libby had been left to entertain herself for a little while and she'd happened to notice a few secluded areas it would be fun to explore during the reception.

Her mind had been wandering back to that thought off and on all afternoon, and seeing Theo in her crisp suit and neatly coiffed hair made her squirm in her seat.

"I now pronounce you husband and wife," the officiant said. "You may kiss the bride."

Everyone erupted in applause as Chet grabbed Penny by the waist and dipped her, then everyone in attendance stood and clapped for the happy couple as they recessed off the dock. The wedding party followed and Theo broke rank on her way up the aisle to give Libby a quick kiss.

"How are you doing, babe?" Libby asked.

"Good," Theo said. "We're going to take some bridal party photos now. I'll find you as soon as we're done."

They kissed again and Libby used her handkerchief to remove a little bit of red lipstick she'd transferred to Theo's lips, then she smiled and swatted her behind. "Have fun."

When the wedding party had gone off to begin their photoshoot and the rest of the attendees started to move away from the lake, Libby's mom asked, "Should we avail ourselves of the open bar?"

"Yes, please," Libby said. "And the *hors d'oeuvre* – I haven't eaten since breakfast and I wasn't the one who spent the whole morning getting ready. I can only imagine how hungry Penny must be."

There was a beautiful outdoor reception area decorated in tiger lilies that complemented the natural greenery of the vineyard. Libby, her mom and Robin got chilled glasses of sangria from the bar and Libby nibbled on cheese and crackers from an elaborate spread of appetizers while they waited for the wedding party to return.

Libby occupied the time by asking rapid-fire questions about Robin and Andie – "Are you official yet?"

being the most important one – but Robin played it cool no matter how much Libby pried.

"We don't want to define it. It's hard to maintain a relationship when there are five hundred miles between us."

"You and I have made a long-distance friendship last for over a decade," Libby pointed out. "If you like each other, you shouldn't let the distance be an obstacle."

"Friendship's different than romance," Robin countered.

"But all good romances include a strong friendship."

"Look who's the expert all of a sudden," Robin teased. "You've been in *one* serious relationship."

"Just because it took me 35 years to find the right woman doesn't mean I don't know anything about love." Libby shoved a cube of cheese in her mouth, then added, "You two are cute together, and you know she didn't *mean* to knock you down while she was drooling over Nat Butler."

Robin rolled her eyes, but she also laughed. "I get it. I'm sure there are some celesbians I would knock Andie over for, and that's what I told her when I apologized for ending our weekend abruptly. If I'm ever in a room with Andie and Kate McKinnon, she owes me a pass."

Libby laughed so hard she almost spit her cheese out, and the three of them lingered near the appetizer spread until she'd had her fill. Then they found a table and sat down to wait.

There were more lilies in a beautifully arranged centerpiece and Penny had spared no detail, from the tidy pouches of Jordan almonds to the salmon-colored napkins folded into hearts on each dinner plate.

"How excited are you to officially retire in a month, Mom?"

Libby's mother took a long, luxurious sip of sangria and smiled. "I can hardly wait."

"What are you going to do with your time?" Robin asked.

"Nothing," she laughed. "Absolutely nothing, at least for the rest of the summer." She ate a peach slice out of her sangria and savored it, then added, "After that, I'm not sure. I've always wanted to do something artistic so maybe I'll take a painting class. I'll still be teaching my workshops at Good Vibes, of course, but when I've got the time, I think I'd like to travel a little bit."

"You've got a couch to crash on if you ever want to come to Toronto," Robin said.

Libby's mom laughed. "Thanks, sweetie, but I think I'm past my couch-crashing days."

"Well, Toronto's got a lot of Airbnb listings," Robin amended. "I'm sure you could find something suitable."

"How are you liking the new apartment?" Libby asked. "Does it feel like home yet?"

"Not quite, but it's nice," her mom said. "The view of the water is exactly what I dreamed of and I've got the rest of my life to make the apartment exactly what I want it to be, so I'm taking my time getting settled in. Speaking of making things how you want them, how are things going at the shop?"

"Really well, actually," Libby said. Now it was her

turn to beam. "I have resolved myself to the fact that I will probably always find a way to screw things up, like forgetting to submit those purchase orders in time for Pride, but I'm actually really good at improvising to make up for it."

"Those tutus sold like hotcakes," her mom agreed.

"Actually, I've got a new idea I've been rolling around in my head lately," Libby said. "I haven't even told Theo yet."

"Told me what?" Right on cue, Theo appeared, resting her hand on the back of Libby's chair.

"All done with photos?" Robin asked.

"The bridal party is," Theo said. "Penny and Chet are still posing for pictures. Andie made a pit stop at the bar but she'll be over in a minute."

"Have a seat," Libby's mom said.

Libby took Theo's hand and pulled her into the chair beside her. Theo scooted closer so she could put her arm around Libby. "So what is it that you haven't told me yet?"

"I was just saying I had an idea that could really solidify Good Vibes in the sex shop industry," Libby answered. She shrugged and added, "Or it could be a total flop, which is why I haven't mentioned it yet."

"Don't sell yourself short, babe. What's the idea?"

"Hand-sewn costumes," Libby said, holding her breath as the three most important people in her life stared back at her.

No one rushed to answer. Were they waiting for more? Better? Was it a colossally stupid idea?

She hurried to expand on her idea. "I've always wished the shop had a bigger footprint because at least once a week, I get exotic dancers and cosplayers who come in and ask where my clothing section is, especially after they notice that I sew my own clothes. And then there are a lot of couples looking for roleplay outfits. I just don't have room to stock a lot of inventory and clothing takes up space. But if I took custom orders, I could focus on just a few at a time with flashy window displays – take orders for costumes that are available for a limited time and tailor them especially for each client…"

She stopped and took a deep breath, suddenly aware that she hadn't inhaled the whole time she was talking.

"Well?" she asked. "What do you think?"

"I love it," her mom said.

"I'd be your first customer," Robin chimed in. "I've always loved your style."

"I think it's perfect," Theo said, and her praise was what brought the biggest smile to Libby's lips.

"It is?"

"Yeah," Theo said. "It's a great match for your skillset and you're a walking billboard for your talents. Plus, no online retailer in the world could compete with something like that. And I've seen how envious some of your clients are when they're admiring your clothes – you definitely have a hungry audience."

Libby let out a long sigh of relief. "So I should do it?"

"Hell yes," all three of them said in unison.

Libby laughed, then stood up. "Another round of sangria on me!"

"It's an open bar," Robin pointed out.

"Don't steal my thunder," Libby shot back with another laugh.

She spent the rest of the reception with a huge smile on her lips. Maybe it was the wine, or the mid-summer breeze coming off the lake, or the fact that she'd suddenly gotten everything she ever wanted.

Penny and Chet came back from their photo session, everyone sat down to eat, and then the dance floor began to fill up as people shed their inhibitions and the reception turned into a lively celebration. Libby even dragged Theo onto the dance floor for the Electric Slide despite her protests.

"I'm not much of a dancer."

"Everyone can slide."

"No, really-"

"You're drunk. Everyone's drunk. It's pretty much *required* that you make a fool of yourself like the rest of us," Libby said, taking her hand and pulling her forcefully to the center of the crowd.

Theo did one self-conscious round of the dance, then she started getting into it. Her inhibitions fell away and Libby spent the rest of the song laughing her ass off while her girlfriend totally rocked the decades-old dance.

"I knew you could slide!" she called over the music. "You're a natural."

A slow song came on after and Theo wrapped her around Libby's waist, holding her close. They did a simple side-to-side sway and Libby asked, "How are you doing?"

"Good," Theo said.

"No anxiety?"

"Not right now. I always feel safer when I'm with you," Theo said. "The ceremony was kind of nerve-wracking, though."

"It didn't show."

"Good."

"So I guess your therapy appointments are helping?"

Libby had talked Theo into attending a few more appointments over the last couple of weeks, even though she liked to ration them throughout the year. Libby had argued that Theo would get more out of each session when she was feeling good, rather than waiting until her anxiety was so bad that just showing up to her therapist's office was a struggle.

So far, it seemed to be working.

"Yeah, and talking to you helps, too," Theo said. "You're one less person I have to put on a mask for. One less person who thinks I'm okay when I'm really just trying to hold it all together."

"You hold it together beautifully, whether you think so or not," Libby said.

"You make it worth the effort," Theo said. "I don't want to hide from life when I get to spend it with you."

"I'm glad."

The song ended and a pop song came on next. Libby saw the reluctance in Theo's face and decided not to torture her with another fast song – at least not now.

She led her off the dance floor and into the converted barn where the bridal party had gotten ready that morning. There was a powder room Libby had her eye on earlier and she hoped to find it empty.

"Where are we going?" Theo asked.

"To hide from life for just a few minutes," Libby said. "It's okay to hide every once in a while."

She gave Theo a wink, then pulled her into the powder room.

21

THEO

By the end of July, Libby had somehow managed to convince Theo to use her mom's most loyal workshop attendees as a focus group to test-drive her game.

Theo spent the entire week beforehand designing and printing fresh copies of her deck, laminating them and putting them together in the nicest presentation she could make in her home office.

She'd surprised even herself with the professionalism of the deck by the time she was done. There were almost a hundred cards, as inclusive as she and Libby could dream up by themselves, and Theo had to admit that even from the subjective perspective of the creator, the game was a lot of fun.

It never played out the same way twice and no one was ever sorry to lose. Best of all, there were plenty of opportunities for her beloved fill-in-the-blank cards, making each deck completely unique.

"Are you ready for this?" Libby asked when Theo showed up at Good Vibes an hour before the workshop. She'd gathered about twenty volunteers and they were all waiting at the back of the shop, where Libby had cleared some space to play.

Theo set a reusable grocery bag full of decks on the counter and came around to give Libby a kiss. "Yeah, I'm actually pretty excited. I hope your customers like the game as much as we do."

"I'm sure they will." Libby stroked her hand down Theo's back and squeezed her cheeks, then asked, "Did you come up with a name yet?"

"Yeah," Theo said, rummaging in the bag. She pulled out one of the decks and handed it to Libby, smiling broadly.

"*Fantasy Foreplay*," Libby read. "Evocative – I like it."

"Thanks," Theo said, then she laughed and took the deck back. "I'm glad you like it because Andie and I spent about three hours folding cardstock into game boxes and I'm not renaming it until at least the second manufacturing run."

"I think it's perfect. Come on, I'll introduce you to your focus group."

Theo slung her bag over her shoulder and followed Libby to the back of the shop. There were two dozen people waiting there and Theo felt a flutter of nervousness in her belly as Libby led her to them.

This is just like leading a conference call with a

client, she told herself. Except she never expected her clients to tell her the passion project she'd been working on for the better part of a year was asinine. And here she was practically begging these strangers to do just that.

They were all sitting cross-legged on blankets, waiting patiently for the focus group to begin.

Most of them had come in pairs, but there were a few who appeared to be flying solo and who looked just as nervous as Theo. Libby plopped down right in the middle of the solo cluster, working her magic to dispel the nervous energy. She was chatty and welcoming, putting everyone at ease, and Theo was grateful because it had the same effect on her.

She took a deep breath. She smiled. And then she introduced herself. "My name is Theo. I'm Libby's girlfriend, but I think you all already knew that from the focus group invitation."

"And because you practically live at Good Vibes," Libby heckled her. A few people laughed and that helped break the ice.

"Guilty as charged," Theo said with a smile. "Well, one apparent side effect of spending so much time in a sex shop is that you start to get some naughty ideas. For the last few months, Libby's been helping me develop a card game for lovers – one that's inclusive of everyone in the LGBT+ community because I don't know if you've looked, but there's not a lot on the market just for us."

"We know!" someone else called out to another round of laughter.

"Well, there is now," Theo said proudly. "Or at least there *will* be as soon as I find a distributor."

She opened her bag and her stomach did an excited little jump as she took out a deck.

"It's called *Fantasy Foreplay*," Theo said. She walked among the blankets to hand out the decks, and Libby popped up to help her.

"You explain how it works," she said. "I'll handle the rest."

She gave Theo a wink and someone cat-called them from the singles section. *Yeah*, Theo thought, *Cora's sex workshop group is the perfect, uninhibited crowd to test the game on.*

She kept one deck for herself and went back to the front of the space, where everyone could see her clearly. She started taking out cards and explaining the rules while Libby made sure everyone got a deck of their own.

"I got 'lick'," the cat-caller announced as she pulled out a few cards. "Who has 'pussy'?"

There were a few chuckles – Theo had the woman pegged for a class clown type – and a redhead sitting in the singles section answered wryly, "I've got one for you."

"Oh, hell, who needs the rest of the game?" the cat-caller joked. "I got what I came for."

"Sounds like you won JT over," Libby said. "But for those of us who aren't natural pick-up artists, you better explain the rest, babe."

"I'm always open to learning a thing or two," JT said, yielding the floor back to Theo but not before giving the redhead one more salacious look.

Theo finished explaining the rules while everyone looked through their decks, then they all paired or grouped up to play a round of the game.

"Please think out loud while you're playing," Theo said. "If you have questions or anything is confusing, I'd love to hear your feedback. Let me know which cards you like, what you think is missing, and any improvements I can make."

She took a notebook out of her bag and walked as unobtrusively as possible through the clusters of people on the blankets while they played. Most of them paired with the partners they'd arrived with, but a few couples banded together, and Libby grouped six singles into a set of playmates.

Theo paid particular attention to the larger groups, observing how the game progressed with more than two players since she and Libby had never expanded beyond the two of them.

"I'm getting left out over here," one of the singles in the big group said after about ten minutes. "We've played three rounds and nobody has picked my action cards so I'm feeling a little like the awkward one at the orgy who can't figure out how to get in there."

"Jump in with your tongue out and your mind open," JT suggested from one blanket over. She was getting cozy with the redhead, but apparently not too cozy to resist the invitation for commentary.

Theo was vaguely aware of another ripple of laughter from the group, but she was too focused on the problem at hand. She nibbled the cap of her pen as she took notes, then said, "So for larger groups, we need to add additional rules or maybe some kind of side action to keep everyone involved."

She jotted down a few notes, then kept circulating. The focus group had all kinds of useful feedback – even the jokester, JT, offered Theo no less than ten creative ideas for additional Action cards. They loved the Heat cards and Theo had several pages of notes by the end of the session.

Once they'd all had a chance to play about half a dozen rounds – and they looked eager to go home and resume the game in private – Theo called everyone's attention.

"Alright, everyone," she said. "This has given me so much to think about and a lot of excellent feedback – thank you so much for coming."

"No, thank *you*," JT said, right on cue, and got the room laughing again.

"You're welcome," Theo shot back. "Those prototype decks are yours to keep, so I hope you continue to enjoy them. If you have any more thoughts or ideas for additional cards, my email address is printed on the back of the box."

She released the group and chose to take it as a compliment when the shop cleared out quickly. Theo noticed JT and the redhead leaving together and when Libby came over and wrapped one arm around Theo's waist, she said, "Looks like at least one love connection was made tonight."

"I guess the game works," Theo said.

"It definitely does," Libby answered. "JT and her playmate were not the only people feeling amorous as they left here tonight. I saw a lot of flushed and smiling faces. You should be proud of yourself – I know I am."

"Proud that your girlfriend is making the queer women of East Village horny?" Theo teased. "You okay with that?"

"I do it every day," Libby pointed out. "Or at least I try. Now we've got a unified mission – call me crazy but it makes me feel closer to you."

"Oh yeah?" Theo said, pulling Libby's hips to hers. "How close?"

Libby indulged her, kissing her and letting her body melt against Theo. She was just getting ready to pull Libby down to the cluster of blankets when Libby stepped back.

"Where are you going?"

"I fully intend on being one of those horny women who gets lucky because of your game tonight," she said, "but first, there's something you need to do."

"What's that?"

"Come on."

Theo followed Libby to the front of the store. Libby made a quick detour to lock the door, then led Theo behind the counter.

"We could leave the lights off," Theo suggested, glancing at the table where she and Libby had made love with the strap-on for the first time. A pulse of desire throbbed between her legs and she pinned Libby against the counter, but Libby was relentless when she had her sights set on something.

"Don't worry, babe," she said. "We'll turn them off soon enough."

Theo bit her lip and pressed her hips against Libby's plump ass. She kissed the curve of her neck while Libby tapped her keyboard, bringing her computer monitor to life.

"What are we doing?" Theo murmured against her skin.

"*You* are applying for an exhibition booth at Sexy-Con," Libby said.

That gave Theo pause. Her lips stilled against Libby's skin and her stomach gave a little jump. "I am?"

"We only have two more months," Libby said. "And you're the one who's all about planning – we can't very well wait so long they run out of spots."

"Two months," Theo said. "That's not much time to make all the changes people suggested tonight *and* find someone who can print the game. Did you see how many notes I took?"

"It doesn't have to be perfect," Libby said, pulling up the SexyCon website. "That's why you're getting an exhibitor booth rather than a vendor booth. *Next* year, you can start selling the game."

"Oh wow," Theo said, suddenly feeling a little lightheaded at the idea of charging people for something she dreamed up in her bedroom. "Do you really think it's good enough?"

"*Yes*," Libby said sternly. "You know damn well it's great, and everyone in the focus group thought so, too. If you can turn on that many people in an awkward public setting, just think how hot they're going to be when they get home and have a chance to play their Fantasy cards."

Theo smiled. It was a good feeling.

Libby slid the keyboard over. "Here – I pulled up the exhibitor application. You got this, babe."

Theo smirked at her. "Since when are you Miss Plan-In-Advance?"

"Since I fucked up my last SexyCon appearance," Libby said, laughing. "I'm not going to let that happen again – I submitted my own exhibitor application three weeks ago to show off the first pieces in my clothing line."

"Well, look at you," Theo teased. She gave Libby a kiss, then put her fingers to the keys. "This is really happening, huh?"

"Yep," Libby said, kissing Theo's neck and running her hands all over her while she typed. "You're going to be famous, at least in the LGBT+ sex games market."

"So, not very famous at all." Theo laughed, then groaned as Libby's hand slid between her thighs. "Do you want me to fill this out or not? Because you're making it hard to remember how to spell my own name."

Libby breathed into Theo's ear, sending shivers down her spine as she whispered, "T-H-E-O. Take your time, but know that I'll be waiting for you upstairs, stark naked, when you're done."

Theo closed her eyes and groaned again as Libby stroked her through her jeans, then Libby's hand disappeared. When she opened her eyes again, Libby had disappeared as well and Theo could hear the stairs leading up to the apartment creaking.

Theo typed faster.

22

LIBBY

Libby's mom had a retirement party at the beginning of August to celebrate the next chapter in her life.

Libby made herself a floral tea dress just for the occasion. Her sewing machine had gotten an awful lot of use over the past few months and she needed all the practice she could get before the launch of her new line in the fall.

"You look beautiful," Theo told her when she met Libby outside Good Vibes. She was holding a bouquet of wildflowers and she didn't look so bad herself in a crisp white button-down and a pair of gray twill shorts. Her cheeks had a certain flush to them that Libby wasn't used to, like she was nervous but not in a panicking way.

"You think so?" Libby asked, spinning so her skirt would catch the breeze.

"Stunning," Theo said, giving her a kiss.

"Are those for me?" Libby nodded at the flowers and Theo looked bashful.

"They're for your mom, actually," she said stumbling on her words a little like when they'd first started dating. "But if you like them, we can pick her up something else on the way to the party."

Libby smiled. "No, I think it's sweet you bought my mom flowers. Just remember you're coming home with me tonight."

Theo laughed and linked her arm in Libby's. "I wouldn't have it any other way."

The day was warm, with a late summer breeze that Libby drank in as soon as they emerged from the subway at their destination on the other side of the city. The party was at a park with a large pavilion and a gazebo that looked out on a glimmering pond. There were at least two dozen people there when Libby and Theo arrived, her mom's friends and Libby's extended family members. They'd decorated the pavilion with elegant bunting and paper lanterns.

"Your flowers are going to go perfect with the motif here," Libby pointed out as she looked around for her mom. She spotted her by the pond and pulled Theo over to her.

"Hi there, sweetie," her mom said. "I'm so glad you both could make it."

"How does it feel to be done with the rat race?" Theo asked, handing her the flowers.

"Oh, these are beautiful! Thank you," she said, inhaling their perfume. "It's a little bittersweet. I'll miss my clients – well, most of them." She chuckled, then smiled. "But it's good to be free to do whatever I like with my time."

Libby's mom pulled each of them into a hug, then Libby said, "I'm so happy for you, Mom."

"And I'm happy for you. I'm proud of all you've accomplished this year," she said. "Both of you, actually."

Libby beamed. "I'm proud of us, too."

"Well, go get yourselves some food!" her mom said. "Your Aunt Rose catered the whole party."

She listed off the foods available – fried chicken, potato wedges, finger sandwiches, and a huge retirement cake bursting with buttercream roses. Libby's mouth was watering by the time they got to the buffet inside the pavilion. She watched Theo walk down the buffet line in front of her, taking tiny portions of everything.

"Not hungry?"

"Not particularly."

"Are you feeling okay?"

"Yeah," Theo said. "I'm fine."

She didn't sound fine, and she wasn't normally one to shy away from good food – at least not since she'd started to get a handle on her anxiety and learn to control the panic reflex. "Is it your agoraphobia? We've never been to this park before."

"Maybe a little," Theo said. "Don't worry about me, though."

That was an impossible request and Theo knew it, but Libby did her best not to harp on the subject. Libby had learned over the last few months that Theo would work through her anxiety in her own time, and the best thing Libby could do was be by her side in case Theo needed her.

"Do you want to eat in the gazebo?" Libby asked. "The water looks so inviting."

"Sure."

Clipped answers were a sure sign that Theo's anxiety was troubling her, but she clearly didn't want to talk about it. So Libby slid her hand into Theo's and they carried their plates over to the empty gazebo. The breeze was stronger there, carried across the pond, and it felt good in the heat of the afternoon.

They ate for a few minutes and Libby made small talk about the relatives she recognized but rarely saw. "We don't have to stay long – my mom's family has never been the social type and I wouldn't know what to say to most of them. I just wanted to make an appearance for my mom's sake."

"We can stay as long as you like, babe," Theo said. "You know, I'm really proud of you, too."

"Hmm?"

"For everything you've done with Good Vibes this year," she said. "And everything you're planning to do next year. You really turned that shop around, and I can already tell your costume line is going to be a smash hit."

"You think so?"

"I know so," Theo said. "Babe, you're a walking advertisement for your skills."

She glanced around, checking to make sure no one was looking their way, then she leaned in and planted a deep kiss on Libby's lips. Libby closed her eyes and she felt Theo's hand sliding discreetly beneath the hem of her skirt. All the nervousness from earlier had suddenly faded away and that simple touch had Libby's heart pounding with desire.

"Theo," Libby objected, pulling away with a smile on her face. "We're going to get caught."

"I can't help myself," Theo murmured, but she pulled her hand away and smoothed Libby's skirt back down over her thigh. "You're irresistible, and I'm sure everyone will think the same about your costumes."

"I take it you're feeling better?"

"A little," Theo said, then finally she confessed, "but I'm nervous because I have a question I've been wanting to ask you."

Libby's heart leaped in her chest. Theo wasn't the type to be coy, and if she was feeling anxious about it, the question had to be serious. But now she was being maddeningly silent.

"Yes?" Libby prompted.

"Not here," Theo said, taking another bite of her sandwich. "This is your mom's moment."

"Tease," Libby said, bumping Theo's shoulder with her own. "Will you tell me when we get back to my place?"

"Let's go to my place instead," Theo suggested. "Andie's visiting Robin this weekend and I've got the place to myself."

"Okay," Libby said. "But just so you know, it's going to kill me to wait that long. I won't be able to stop wondering what the question is."

"I'm sorry."

"No you're not," Libby said with a laugh.

And she didn't forget. There were gifts and cake. Libby's aunt made a moving speech about her baby sister entering a new and exciting phase of her life. Libby's mom teared up and thanked everyone for being there. And the moment the crowd began to thin out, Libby asked Theo, "Are you ready to go?"

"Whenever you are, babe."

"And then you'll ask your question?"

Theo laughed. "It's been eating you alive, hasn't it?"

"Even more than the mosquitoes," Libby said. They went back to the pavilion, where Libby's mom and aunt were beginning to take down the decorations. Libby hugged her mom and said, "Congratulations again on your retirement."

"Thank you, sweetie," she said, looking up from a pile of bunting. "Are you two heading out?"

"We were thinking about it," Libby said. "We're more than happy to help you clean up if you want, though."

"Nah, I've got a whole army of helpers," her mom said. "You two enjoy the rest of your weekend. Do you want to take some food to go, though?"

"No, that's okay. You should keep it."

"It won't all fit in my fridge," her mom countered. "Take some chicken at least."

Libby knew there was no way they were leaving without some leftovers. Theo laughed and said her mom was the same way. "You don't leave the Kostas house until you're at least ten pounds heavier than when you came in. Whether it's in your belly or in a Tupperware container, it's all the same to my mom."

Libby's mom laughed, then sent them home with two aluminum chafing dishes full of leftovers. As Theo struggled to carry them on the subway, Libby tried to apologize but Theo just shrugged.

"All moms are the same," she said. "Mine would have probably sent us home with the whole buffet."

BY THE TIME they got to Theo's apartment building, Libby had become a complete and utter pest about Theo's unspoken question.

"We're ten steps from your place," she said in the hallway. "You can just tell me now."

"Nope." Theo had a big grin on her face, clearly enjoying the game.

"Come on," Libby said. "It's not *that* big a question, is it?"

In fact, Theo was starting to freak her out a little bit. Libby had pestered her about it at first because it was fun, but the more Theo refused to budge, the more Libby wondered what Theo wanted to ask her.

It couldn't be... *the* question... right?

They'd never even discussed marriage and while Libby's heart already belonged to Theo forever, she couldn't imagine her asking that question on a random day and completely out of the blue.

But the more Theo built it up...

"You're killing me," Libby protested.

"Eight more steps," Theo said. When they got to the door, she paused and tried to juggle the chafing dishes into one hand.

"Want me to hold those?"

"Nah," Theo said. "Just get my keys out of my front pocket."

She shifted the dishes out of the way and Libby caught a slight smirk on Theo's lips. "What?"

"Just get my keys," Theo said. "Hurry, this chicken is heavy."

Libby put her hand in Theo's pocket, expecting to find her keyring and touching something flat and rubbery instead. She knit her brows and Theo nodded, so she pulled it out.

"What is this?" she asked. It was a tan balloon that obviously had Theo's apartment key stuffed inside of it. "Theo, you are one strange individual."

Theo cracked a smile, then shook her head. "This did *not* go how I wanted it to. Leave it to your mom to load me down with so much food I could barely carry it all. Trade me for a second, okay? This'll make more sense in a minute."

She passed the chafing dishes to Libby and took the balloon from Libby. Theo blew it up and Libby laughed when it took shape. It was a booby balloon. "You kept those from your first time in my shop?"

"Just this one," Theo said. "Don't ask me why, but I had some crazy intuition that it might come in handy again someday."

Libby couldn't help laughing and Theo traded her again before she could drop the chafing dishes. She took them and gave the balloon to Libby.

"If Andie hadn't bought the booby balloons, she never would have left her phone at your shop-"

"Best booby trap ever," Libby interjected.

"-and I probably never would have set foot in Good Vibes again. Really, when you think about it, our entire relationship developed thanks to those balloons."

"Aww." It sounded cheesy as hell on the surface, but Libby was swooning.

"I've been working really hard on myself and getting my anxiety under control," Theo said. "I want to move in with you as soon as it makes sense, but in the meantime, I want you to feel just as at home at my place as you are in your apartment. The key inside the balloon is a copy I had made for you. I know it's a small step, but I *do* want to take the next step in our relationship. And the next, and the next."

Libby smiled. "Really?"

"Absolutely," Theo said. "I'm not whole without you by my side."

"Theo, I love you so much." Libby wrapped her arms around her and Theo nearly dropped the chafing dishes. "Oh shit, sorry."

"Get your new key out of there and give it a whirl," Theo said. "This food's getting heavy."

Libby let the balloon deflate with a long squeak, then pulled the key out and opened the apartment door. While Theo went into the kitchen and put the food in the refrigerator, Libby turned the key over in her hand and asked, "Is Andie cool with this?"

"Oh yeah, she loves you," Theo said. "She said, and I quote, 'Mi casa es su casa, as long as you don't do any more freaky shit with the pot holders'."

Libby cracked up, then Theo came over and wrapped her in her arms.

"So?" she asked. "Was that the world's dorkiest way to give you a key to my place?"

Libby laughed. "Yes, definitely. But I loved it."

"And I love you, Libby," Theo said. "Now get in my bed. I told you that dress was driving me crazy."

EPILOGUE
THEO

If Theo found SexyCon overwhelming the previous year, its crowds were nothing compared to the long line of people wrapped around the convention center the following September, waiting for the doors to open.

"Holy crap," was the first thing out of her mouth as she got out of Cora's car and saw them all. "What happened?"

"Buzz," Libby said, coming around the back of the car and giving Theo's ass a teasing pinch. "Word on the street is that SexyCon got a ton of attention in the mainstream press this year."

"So much the better for you two," Cora said, popping the trunk. "Let's get you set up."

This year, they were staying for all three days of the convention and they'd brought an entire car full of merchandise, a couple of huge banners for their exhibition booths, and a litany of swag – everything from stickers to magnets and business cards. Libby had managed to stuff two dress forms into the car and Theo had shared the back seat with them during the long drive.

The three of them grabbed as much as they could carry and headed into the convention center through the vendor entrance. The building wasn't nearly as crowded as the sidewalk outside – SexyCon's doors wouldn't open to the public for another two hours – but there was a definite hum of excitement inside as the vendors and exhibitors got their booths set up.

"My booth is over here," Libby said, pointing down one aisle in the crowded exhibitor hall. "Theo, yours is in Aisle D, right?"

"Yeah," she said. "But I don't have much to set up. I'll help you for a while."

All Theo needed to demonstrate *Fantasy Foreplay* was her banner, the business cards she'd had hastily printed off, and the game itself. She'd managed to get a small run of decks made by a mom and pop print shop in Brooklyn and she had about a hundred of them to sell at SexyCon.

She was still not entirely confident that she'd sell a single deck, but Libby was insistent that she'd sell out on the first day.

"Thanks, babe," Libby said. "I could use all the help I can get!"

And she really could. It took three trips to carry all her costumes and swag in from the car, and another hour to get it all arranged in her booth. When Theo, Libby and Cora stepped back to admire their handiwork, she had to admit it was worth all those trips. The booth was an explosion of rainbow colors and enticing costumes sure to turn every head that walked past it.

"Oh, sweetie, it looks so good!" Cora said. "You're going to get a *lot* of traffic with an eye-catching display like this."

The two dress forms were set up right at the front of Libby's booth, both decked out in rainbow-colored costumes. She had a selection of other costumes hanging from clothing rods behind the table, and a tie-dyed tablecloth was already drawing the other exhibitors' eyes to her display.

"I hope so," Libby said. "Theo, what about you? We spent so much setup time on me. Let's get your booth in shape."

Theo accepted the help, although her setup process amounted to laying out an identical tie-dyed tablecloth – Libby had insisted on making it for her as her contribution to Theo's booth – and spreading business cards and game instruction sheets across the table. After they hung Theo's banner, Cora checked the time.

"Ten minutes til the doors open," she said. "You two ready for this?"

Libby looked to Theo, that old familiar expression in her eyes. It was an unspoken question, *Are you okay?* and lately, the answer was always *yes*.

"I'm ready as I'll ever be," Theo said.

"I just need to get changed," Libby answered, throwing a garment bag over her shoulder. She took Theo's hand. "Come with me, babe. We probably won't get to see much of each other today so I want every last minute I can get."

Theo followed Libby to the restroom while Cora kept an eye on their booths. If they'd planned a little further in advance, it would have been nice to get exhibition spaces that were side by side – but there was always next year. In the meantime, Cora had volunteered to act as both Libby and Theo's gopher, circulate back and forth between the two booths in case either of them needed a snack, a bathroom break, or anything else.

For now, Theo was happy to stick with Libby and enjoy a quiet moment of calm before the chaos that was SexyCon.

They went into the restroom at the back of the exhibition room. There was a dressing area immediately inside the door and toilet stalls around the corner, and it seemed that for the moment, they had the space to themselves.

Libby hung her garment bag from a hook on the wall and took out her costume for the day – a brightly-colored tutu that was a refined version of the one she'd made for Pride, along with a custom-sewn bodice and a pair of go-go boots that would probably have her feet aching by the end of the day. To crown it all, she'd brought the fuzzy cat ears from her childhood bedroom that had started it all.

Theo watched Libby get changed out of her jeans, pulling the tutu on over a pair of rainbow-colored Spandex shorts. Then she took off her t-shirt and tossed it at Theo with a wink.

"Lace me up?" she asked as she held the bodice over her chest.

She turned her back to Theo, who did as Libby asked, looking over her shoulder and admiring her in the full-length mirror on the wall.

The bodice had a push-up effect on her breasts and when Libby caught Theo looking, she grinned. "What do you think?"

"I think you're the sexiest woman alive," Theo said. "And I think you're going to come home after the convention with about a thousand purchase orders."

"That's the idea," Libby said, satisfied.

Theo finished lacing the bodice, then wrapped her arms around Libby's waist, already hungry for her even though they had a long day ahead of them. She kissed her jaw, then nibbled her neck. "You're irresistible."

"You'll have to try," Libby said, turning and running her hand down to Theo's hip. "We better get back out there."

THE FIRST DAY of SexyCon was a complete whirlwind. If it wasn't for Cora's help, Theo wouldn't have remembered to eat, and if it wasn't for Libby, she wouldn't have been bold enough to call attention to her booth.

After the first hour, Libby asked her mom to hold down the fort at her booth so she could check on Theo. She came down Aisle D and found her sitting patiently behind her tie-dyed table, waiting for people to notice her as attendees streamed past.

"Babe!" Libby said. "What are you doing?"

"Umm, manning my booth?"

"You gotta command attention," she said, coming pulling Theo to her feet. "Get out in the aisle and steer people to your table."

"I don't-"

Before Theo could mount a protest, Libby shoved her into the stream of people walking through the exhibition hall. They all had swag bags looped over their arms and most of them had that hungry look in their eyes, like they were on the hunt for something, *anything* that was free.

"Hey! You wanna explore your fantasies?" Libby shouted at the nearest passers-by, a couple holding hands as they walked.

"You offering to help?" one of them asked and her partner smacked her in the chest. Libby didn't miss a beat – she guided them both over to Theo's table and shoved business cards into their hands.

"Tell them about the game, babe."

"Umm," Theo stuttered, her mind going blank for just a second.

Libby was a natural at drawing people in, making them feel at home, and Theo wouldn't be the least bit surprised if she'd already taken at least one purchase order in the first hour of the convention. That outgoing, natural enthusiasm wasn't Theo's style, but she knew enough about marketing to know she couldn't spend the next three days waiting to be noticed.

She recovered from the momentary brain fart before Libby finished distributing instruction sheets for the game and told the couple about *Fantasy Foreplay*. By the time they left the booth, Theo had made her first sale – in no small part thanks to Libby – and she looked at her girlfriend in awe.

"You're so good at this."

"You just gotta get a little bit loud and show people you have something worth paying attention to," Libby said. "I need to get back to the Good Vibes booth. You got this?"

"I got this," Theo said. Libby kissed her and Theo watched her tutu sway as she disappeared into the crowd. Then she took a deep breath and flagged down the next couple heading her way, pulling them toward her table with the same pick-up line Libby had used. "Want to explore your fantasies?"

It worked – and it worked well.

By the end of the day, Theo had only about twenty-five decks left and she'd blown through all her business cards in the first three hours. She was just making calculations about how many more she'd have to order to have enough for all three days of next year's convention when she spotted Libby coming back up the aisle, a swag bag looped over her arm.

She was still wearing her costume and Theo admired the way those go-go boots hugged her calves and lengthened her legs.

"Hey, babe," Libby said. "You ready to get out of here?"

"Sure. Where's Cora?"

"Attending an evening workshop," Libby said. "We've got the evening all to ourselves."

"Is that so?" Theo wrapped one arm around Libby's waist, pulling her into a kiss. "What should we do with it?"

"I have one idea," Libby said. "Let's go check out our hotel room. Maybe order room service?"

"Sounds good to me," Theo said.

They packed up everything essential – including Theo's small stack of unsold *Fantasy Foreplay* decks and the fifteen purchase orders Libby had taken – and wandered through the convention center to the adjoining hotel.

Theo and Libby had gotten a room together and Cora was staying down the hall. Thank God for that, because Theo couldn't keep her hands off Libby for another second – not after an entire day of high adrenaline, sexy conversations going on all around her, and that irresistible bodice.

Libby was on exactly the same page. The moment Theo closed their hotel door, she put her hands on her hips and commanded, "Get into bed."

Theo gave her a challenging look. "You're pretty bossy tonight."

"I know what I want."

"And that is?"

"You," she said, her eyes following Theo on her way to the bed. Libby bit her lip, then held out the swag bag.

"I got something for us to try," she said. "If you're up for it."

"What is it?"

Libby pulled out a coil of silk rope and let the swag bag drop to the floor. "The girl in the booth across from mine sells bondage equipment on Etsy. She really liked the French maid costume I had hanging on the wall, so I brokered a trade."

Libby uncoiled the rope and Theo grinned at her. "You want me to tie you up?"

"No," Libby said, cracking the rope like a whip. "The opposite, actually."

Theo's stomach gave a quick jump and she took a deep breath. Tied down, unable to escape, completely at Libby's mercy? Her pulse started racing.

"Only if you want to," Libby said. "And we'll pick a safe word in case you want to stop." She came slowly over to Theo, dragging the rope behind her and then running it up Theo's bare arm. It was soft but sturdy and it sent a shiver up Theo's spine. "So, what do you think?"

"Walther," Theo said.

"What?"

"The interactive art exhibition you took me to on our first date," Theo said. "That was the artist's name, wasn't it?"

Libby laughed. "That's our safe word?"

"Well, I definitely won't say it by accident."

"Okay," Libby said, pushing Theo onto the bed. "Walther it is. I have a feeling the artist would approve. Now strip."

Libby stood over Theo and watched every movement as she unbuttoned her shirt, then peeled off her bra. Theo shimmied out of her jeans and Libby teased her bare thighs with the end of the rope as she pulled down her underwear.

"Are you going to get naked, too?"

"In good time," Libby answered with a coy smile. "Scoot up the bed – all the way up to the headboard."

Theo looked behind her. It was a stroke of good luck that the hotel had headboards with slats – or perhaps it had been a conscious choice on the part of the SexyCon planners to select a location with beds suited to their playful audience.

In any case, Theo went obediently to the head of the bed and waited for Libby to join her. She set down the rope for a moment, putting one foot up on the edge of the bed and slowly unzipping her go-go boot. She made a theatrical display of it and every second she made Theo wait, she wanted Libby more.

Slowly, agonizingly, Libby put her bare foot down and repeated the teasing process with the other boot. She peeled off her shorts, then finally, she picked up the rope and stepped onto the bed.

She walked across it, making seductive eye contact with Theo and licking her lips. It was all Theo could do to keep from grabbing Libby and pulling her into her arms. But she waited patiently and was rewarded when Libby sat down in her lap.

"Unlace me," she ordered.

Theo obliged, pulling at the bodice strings behind

Libby's back. It loosened and dropped down around her waist, freeing her gorgeous, full breasts. Theo put her hands on them, bowing her head with the strong desire to take those pert nipples into her mouth, but Libby grabbed her by the wrists.

She pulled them over Theo's head, gave her a tender kiss, and proceeded to tie Theo's hands to the headboard.

"Lie down, babe."

She stood up again, tossing the bodice aside, and Theo shimmied down until she was on her back, arms tied above her head. Libby straddled her hips and the view was fucking incredible.

Theo's eyes bounced back and forth between the curves of Libby's bare breasts, her pert little nipples, and best of all, the damp spot blooming on her panties. Theo could see just a hint of Libby's folds and already she was straining against the rope, craving her wetness.

She was breathing heavy by the time Libby stepped out of her panties and gave Theo the full view she was after. What happened next could well have been written on one of Theo's Fantasy cards.

Libby walked up the bed, then lowered herself over Theo's face. "Eat me, babe."

Theo lifted her head, tongue outstretched as she sought Libby's body. This was what she'd been fantasizing about all day long and Libby had found a way to make it a thousand times better than what Theo had imagined.

Her hands strained against the ropes. Her hips

moved with desire. Her whole body sought Libby and yet she was pinned, completely at Libby's will.

Theo took one long stroke through Libby's folds with her tongue and felt Libby shiver against her mouth. She sat down a little more and Theo buried her face in her girlfriend's wetness, eager to please. Libby's thighs shook and soon she was clutching the headboard, moaning to the ceiling and moving her hips in time with Theo's tongue.

"Oh, fuck yes," she breathed, riding Theo and rocking her hips over her face. Theo kept straining against the silk ropes. She desperately wanted to touch Libby, to run her hands up and down her gorgeous body and slide her fingers into that wetness to make her scream.

All she had was her tongue, though, and it forced her to focus entirely on the only tool available to her. She used it in every creative way she could think of, teasing and lapping at Libby. And it was working. Libby came hard after just a couple minutes, her thighs clamping and shaking against Theo's head.

"Oh, wow," she moaned as her body spasmed and Theo kept lapping at her juices. "Oh, that was so good, babe."

Libby rolled off her, panting, and Theo thought she would untie her. Instead, Libby turned around and slid one hand between Theo's legs. That little touch, after being denied everything except the use of her tongue, was more powerful than anything Theo had felt in a long time.

Her hips were already rising to meet Libby's hand for more, but she pulled back. She grabbed the loose end of the long rope and used it to bind Theo's ankles to the footboard, her legs spread-eagle.

Then Libby straddled Theo's head again, this time facing the foot of the bed.

Theo felt Libby's breath hot against her thighs. She could practically feel her lips brushing her skin, but Libby held back. Instead, she settled her own hips over Theo's mouth, the directive clear enough even without words – *again*.

Theo raised her head to reach her, and the moment her mouth found Libby's clit, Libby brought her mouth down to Theo. She stroked and circled Theo's clit with her tongue and for a moment, Theo's own mouth was frozen in ecstasy. Then an explosion of warmth erupted between her thighs.

She shivered, her legs stiffening as an early ripple of pleasure worked its way through her. Then Libby lowered herself a little more, reminding her what she wanted, and Theo had to split her attention between the incredible pleasure building between her thighs and the glistening folds in front of her face.

Multi-tasking had never been so difficult.

Libby stroked her fingers up and down Theo's wetness then slipped them inside her, and Theo kept rolling her tongue over Libby's clit exactly how she liked it.

Libby came first, already primed and ready, then she

crawled down the bed and focused all of her attention on Theo.

She closed her eyes and relaxed into the moment. What choice did she have? All four of her limbs were tied to the bed. Libby kept fingering her and lapping at her juices, bringing Theo closer and closer to the point of no return.

When Theo's thighs started to quiver, Libby reached down and quickly untied the ropes holding her ankles. Theo brought her knees up, her body contracting around Libby's fingers, and that was all she needed to tip over the edge.

She came harder than she had in a long time, squeezing Libby between her thighs. Libby kept moving her fingers, pumping in and out of her as she teased out a long, intense orgasm. And when Theo finally relaxed, Libby crawled up beside her and curled up against her, wrapping an arm around Theo's middle.

"What did you think?" she asked, tracing one finger over the rope still binding Theo's wrists.

"I liked it," Theo said. "I didn't think I would, but I trust you so it was fun."

"I'm glad."

"And I *definitely* want a turn tying you up."

"I can't wait," Libby said, releasing the rope and freeing her hands. Theo gave her wrists a little shake, then wrapped her arms around Libby.

"I love you so much."

"I love you, too."

Theo kissed her, then let her hand travel slowly down Libby's chest and over her stomach.

"Again?"

"Why not?" Theo asked. "We have all night."

She got on her hands and knees, intent on taking charge of the ropes this time. When she had Libby's hands tied in front of her like handcuffs, she tugged on the rope to pull Libby upright and kissed her. Then she asked, "Will you move in with me?"

"Really?"

"Yeah," Theo said. "I'm ready. I don't want to be apart from you for another minute of my life."

Libby grinned. "What about Andie?"

"She gives us her blessing. I wouldn't be surprised if she ended up moving to Toronto to chase your best friend," Theo said. "She'll be just fine."

"In that case, I would love to live with you, babe."

"And I would love to get you all tied up," Theo said, reaching for Libby's ankles. "Are you ready to explore your fantasies?"

"I'm all yours."

"And I'm yours. Always."

The End

Play Theo's Game!

Fantasy Foreplay is a steamy card game for sapphic lovers. The object is simple - tease and tantalize your playmate until their toes curl!

Explore each other's bodies and let the tension build as you take turns pleasuring each other. The last one to climax is rewarded with a taste of your own personal fantasy...

Download and play now for free

Printed in Great Britain
by Amazon